Gunfire echoed on every side

He paused in shadow, ready for his last spring over weed-choked ground. He took the detonator from his pocket. Bolan still had seven fist-sized C4 charges planted at strategic points throughout the ancient city. None of them had been adjacent to the hiding places of his comrades when the shooting started, and he'd shown the others where they were, in case the natives had to move as he had done. They should be safe—assuming they were still alive—but Bolan couldn't track them down and check.

Choosing the packet farthest from him, on the north rim of the site, he sent a signal beaming through the night and watched it blow. An orange blossom of flame unfurled its petals, searing anyone within a radius of twenty feet and spraying stony shrapnel.

Bolan didn't know if anyone had been within the C4's killing range, and he had no time to investigate the blast site.

He was too busy lighting up the town.

MACK BOLAN ®

The Executioner

The Executioner®
Don Pendleton's
PRIMAL LAW

A GOLD EAGLE BOOK FROM
W☰RLDWIDE®

TORONTO • NEW YORK • LONDON
AMSTERDAM • PARIS • SYDNEY • HAMBURG
STOCKHOLM • ATHENS • TOKYO • MILAN
MADRID • WARSAW • BUDAPEST • AUCKLAND

First edition July 2007

ISBN-13: 978-0-373-64344-8
ISBN-10:   0-373-64344-6

Special thanks and acknowledgment to
Mike Newton for his contribution to this work.

PRIMAL LAW

The only lesson history has taught us is that man has not yet learned anything from history.

—Anonymous

Learning from history doesn't mean that I can change the future, but it's worth a try. In either case, the outcome should be interesting.

—Mack Bolan

For Professors Ian Graham and David Stuard

Prologue

"How much farther?" Howard Travis asked.

He hated that his voice sounded so old and tired, but there it was. At fifty-eight years old, he knew he had no business slogging through the jungle as if he were twenty-five years younger. He was verging on complete exhaustion, covered head-to-foot with bites and stings from a variety of foul, blood-sucking insects, and this morning he felt slightly feverish, but he pressed on.

What other option did he have?

The guide pondered his question, chewing on an unlit corncob pipe that never seemed to leave his mouth, even when they were sharing meager rations by the campfire. Ageless features drooped into a frown, as if the question irritated him somehow, while his protracted silence forced Travis to wonder if the Indian would even deign to answer.

"Few more hours," the guide replied at last, shifting his pipe from the left corner of his wide mouth to the right.

"That's what you told me over breakfast. Now it's almost noon," Travis reminded him.

"A little more. Not long."

"How far in *miles?*" Travis demanded.

With a careless shrug, the guide answered, "Don't know."

The first pulse of a headache throbbed behind his weaker eye, the right. Travis suppressed an urge to rub his temple, likewise biting off the stream of insults that his caustic wit had lined up on the flight deck of his mind, ready to fly if he unleashed them. There was nothing to be gained—and much, potentially, to lose—by pissing off the native help.

"Then tell me this, please, if you can." Travis was justly proud of the control he exercised over his voice. "Do you believe we'll reach the site today?"

"Oh, sure." The Indian seemed confident. "No sweat."

No sweat?

Travis swallowed a yelp of bitter laughter. He was sitting on a log, beside a game trail in the hellish Guatemalan jungle, with three Indians who might be headhunters for all he knew. It was their seventh day of trekking through the godforsaken wilderness—a Friday, if his memory still served him—and for all he knew they had been wandering in circles, wasting precious time and money while the guide and porters had a secret laugh at his expense.

"Six days, you said. This is the seventh."

The Indian turned toward him and cocked an eyebrow. Travis almost reached for his revolver—deadweight on his hip, a hedge against wild animals and never fired—but caught himself. He wasn't Wyatt Earp and stood no realistic chance against the three young men if they decided it was time for him to die. They wouldn't even have to touch him. They could simply melt away into the jungle, leaving him to wander on his own until he dropped.

"Rain slows us down," the guide observed, as if Travis could somehow manage to forget the outpourings from heaven that had drenched them to the skin no less than half a dozen times per day since they had left what passed for civilization in those parts.

"I understand that, but—"

"I tell you in Flores, wet season make it hard, but you say, 'Must go now.' Remember?"

"Yes, of course. I'm simply asking how much longer it should be until we reach the site," Travis said.

"Maybe camp there tonight," the Indian replied.

"Tonight? You're sure?"

"If nothing slows us down."

Travis rose, invigorated with new energy. He still felt slightly feverish and tottered beneath the weight of his backpack, but he blamed it on his excitement. To hell with flies, mosquitoes and the rest, he thought. If they were *that* close to the site, Travis knew he could make it. He would see his dream come true.

"Come on, then," he demanded of his three companions. "Let's get moving! There's no time to waste."

The guide rose slowly, every movement letting Travis know that time meant little to him and meant nothing to the jungle. The porters waited for the guide, then stood in stoic silence with their loads.

They hate me, Travis thought. It was an old tradition in the Latin countries, taking money from the gringos, all the while despising them. Travis could hardly blame them, after all the grief that Guatemala had endured courtesy of Uncle Sam, over the past half-century, but he had tried to make them understand that he had come for *their* sakes, more than for his own.

And it was true—up to a point, at least, he thought. His mission, while it would benefit Travis, would have even greater rewards for Guatemala and her people, for their precious history. If he could find what he was looking for, report it to the government and to the world at large, he could prevent despoliation of a treasure that would surpass all others found within the nation's borders up to now. Travis himself would earn a place in history, of course, but generations yet unborn would thank him for uncovering and safeguarding their timeless heritage.

Sadly, he wouldn't be in time to save it all. Travis wouldn't have known about the site, would never have come searching for it, if the looters hadn't found it first. If it was still unknown, untouched by greedy men, he would be back at Princeton, teaching archaeology to students who were either bored or clueless, going through the motions while he waited for retirement, each day just the same as those that went before.

The quest had changed all that, and he would be forever grateful for the startling diversion, the adventure that had come to him so late in life. Nothing in Travis's experience could match what he had done and seen these past six days—now seven—and he thought it might be worth the effort even if he didn't reach his goal.

But they were close now. He could feel it in his bones.

They had been marching on a vague northeastern course from Flores, toward the border of Belize. Through all of it—the rain, insects and snakes, fatigue that made him want to lie down in the mud regardless of the weather or the hour—Travis had endured. He had surprised himself, and would amaze those who had tried to talk him out of making the attempt. The head of his department had been skeptical, some of his colleagues frankly rude in their dismissal of his scheme, but it was Travis's sabbatical to use as he saw fit. It pleased him to imagine how their jaws would drop when he returned in triumph.

Or perhaps he'd simply tell them that he wasn't coming back. Maybe he'd blow them off, submit early retirement papers and devote himself to working at the site. His pension should be more than adequate to keep a roof over his head in Guatemala, keep his stomach filled with rice and beans while he delved into mysteries as yet unknown.

I just might do that, Travis told himself.

But first, he had to find Site X.

THE TWO-WAY RADIO crackled with static before a tinny voice emerged. "Sierra Bravo calling base. Over?"

It's about damned time, Paco Alvarez thought. His breakfast, powdered eggs with monkey meat, had long since been digested. It was nearly midday. The men were growing restless, double-checking weapons, sharpening their knives, while they killed time and waited for the order to move out.

Alvarez took the walkie-talkie from his web belt, raised it to his lips and thumbed the square transmitter button.

"Speak to me, Sierra Bravo," he commanded. "Over."

"Break time's over," said the voice he recognized as young Juanito's. "They're moving again. Over."

"Direction? Over."

"Still the same, Chief. Northeast. No change. Over."

"Stay with them, but don't show yourselves. We're coming now. Over and out."

He gave Juanito no chance to reply. The youth loved radios and would have kept Alvarez chatting while the batteries ran down and died, if given half a chance. Alvarez snapped an order at his troops and watched them rise as one, ready for the word that would dispatch them on the next leg of their hunt.

Alvarez gave it, turned his back on them and led the way. He was familiar with the jungle, skilled enough to hold a good northeastern course and certain that he would have to kill the men he followed. It seemed that they were not lost, after all. And that, in turn, meant they had to die.

Alvarez didn't know the men he meant to kill. One was American, the others Indians. They meant nothing to him. They could die easily or badly. It would be their choice, after he got some basic information from the American.

Alvarez needed to know why the man was here. Not what he sought—that much was obvious. It was the reason that he had been marked to die. Alvarez was interested in the means by which the stranger had discovered where to look. In all of Guatemala, all the world, what clue had brought him here to find his death?

He might not wish to speak, but Alvarez was confident that he could loosen any tongue, given sufficient time and motivation. Each man had a breaking point. The trick was to find it, exploit weaknesses that might be hidden even from the man himself. In most cases, brute force would do the trick, but sometimes it required a measure of finesse. Whatever method Alvarez was forced to use, he knew he had the strength, the patience and experience to get what he required.

And once he had that information in his hands—what then? Perhaps there would be someone else to silence, maybe several others who had managed to work out the secret. Once he learned their names, if they were anywhere within his reach, Alvarez knew he had to eliminate them too.

But if they were beyond his reach, what could he do? Nothing.

It irritated Alvarez to think of failure. He had grown accustomed to slow progress in the revolutionary movement that consumed his life, was even willing to admit that he might not survive to witness victory. But losing still produced a bitter rage within him, eating at his gut.

Don't worry, urged a small voice in his mind. Americans are easy.

"Some Americans," he muttered to himself, then glanced around to see if any of the soldiers following behind had heard him. None regarded him with anything approaching curiosity, and most were concentrating on the jungle that surrounded them—watching for vipers, jumping spiders, tree roots that could trip them as they marched along. If anyone had heard him speak aloud, he couldn't spot the eavesdropper.

Careful, Alvarez thought. They'll think you've lost your mind.

His temper was ferocious, almost legendary, but if Alvarez's soldiers thought he was insane, some might desert him. That, in turn, would force him to explain the loss and place his own command in jeopardy. Better to simply bite his tongue next time he felt like talking out of turn, and let the argument rage on inside his head.

A fer-de-lance spilled from the undergrowth onto the trail in front of him. Before the snake could form a striking coil,

Alvarez reached out with his rifle, slid the muzzle underneath one fat coil of its body, and flung it far into the jungle with a wrist-flick of disdain. He didn't glance back at the men that time, content to know that some had seen him and would spread the story of his calm contempt for sudden death.

Of such things was a legend made.

Still moving, Alvarez reached out to check his weapon's muzzle, making sure it wasn't fouled with mud or rotting vegetation. When he needed it, he didn't want the weapon to explode and shred his face or hands. There would be risk enough confronting their opponents, without any self-inflicted jeopardy.

What risk, the small voice asked, from an American and three poor Indians?

The problem was that Alvarez had no idea who he was dealing with. The Yankee might be just another bumbling scientist who'd come to make himself a footnote in some journal no one ever read—or he might represent the CIA. In that case, Alvarez and his superiors would have to rethink their basic strategy, seek new and different angles of attack before they walked into a trap and saw the whole world blow up in their faces.

But he didn't think the man he stalked was CIA. He was too old, for one thing, and too soft. As for the Indians, they were hired help and nothing more. Their deaths would prompt no uprising, no government inquiry. They were excess baggage, perfectly disposable.

He wanted the American.

And Alvarez would have him. Soon.

TRAVIS WAS on the verge of calling for another break, fearing he might collapse with his next step or certainly the next one after that, when suddenly his guide let out a whoop and turned to face him with a broad smile on his normally impassive face.

The archaeologist lurched forward, startled by the Indian's

behavior and intent on learning what had caused it. With the question on his lips, he glanced beyond the guide, across the Indian's left shoulder.

He froze. "My God!"

"Not yours," the Indian replied. "Maybe my ancestors or someone else. No white gods here."

It took the archaeologist another beat to get the joke. He snorted a laugh. Impulsively, he squeezed the guide's shoulder, then pushed on past him, brushing ferns and vines aside to get a better view.

An ancient temple stood before him, weathered by the centuries and camouflaged by a bewildering variety of plants that climbed its sloping walls, sprouted from cracks and crevices, or simply clung to scarred and pitted stone. A tree was growing at the very pinnacle, while moss and lichen helped disguise the temple's bas-relief details. But nothing could completely mask its hulking pyramid shape.

And it was not alone.

Awestruck, Travis surveyed the ruins of the city spread before him, as if rising from the jungle or subsiding into it, being devoured or regurgitated inch by inch. The pyramid had clearly been its largest structure, ringed by other buildings, some of which had partially collapsed. He guessed that closer searching would show others that had crumbled down to their foundations over time. What secrets lay in store for him! What wealth, what fame, what—

Travis caught himself, breathed deeply, slowly, to suppress the sudden dizziness he felt. There was a certain protocol to follow with discoveries and excavations. He was merely scouting at the moment, not at all prepared for surveys of the site at large, much less an excavation of the pyramid or its surrounding structures. It might take six months to simply map the city, plot its streets and buildings, without even entering a single one of them.

Elation draining from him, Travis suddenly felt old. He

didn't want to wait six months, had no desire to fill out papers in quadruplicate, debating all the while with government idiots whose first concern would be cashing in—disguised as caring for their nation's history. He longed to race across the open ground in front of him and penetrate the looming pyramid, unlock its secrets immediately.

He wanted to be Indiana Jones.

The notion nearly made him laugh out loud. An actor even older than himself might pull it off with help from stuntmen and computer graphics, but Howard Travis knew his limitations.

Still….

If this was finally the place he sought, then it had been desecrated. He was only there because of looters. He had to prevent them from returning, stealing even more and funneling their loot into the international black market.

What would it hurt to have a look around the place? he wondered.

Surely he'd earned that much, at least.

Travis convinced himself with silent arguments. The site had stood abandoned for some fourteen hundred years. Looters had been the most recent visitors, after a host of jungle insects, birds and animals, perhaps other wandering Indian tribes. What fresh damage could Travis inflict, beyond that already suffered from time and the elements?

"Wait here," he told his guide. "I'll call you if I need you."

"Sí, jefe."

Travis moved cautiously on his approach to the temple. He expected rats and lizards in abundance, which meant snakes and other predators should also be nearby. He hadn't come this far only to let a viper take him out before he had a look around the place.

Site X.

The symbol of enduring mystery. X marks the spot.

And he had found it.

The pyramid was relatively small, no more than sixty feet

between ground level and the tree-topped pinnacle. Up there, he knew, a team of priests had offered human sacrifices to their gods. Some of the victims had been volunteers, although the great majority were prisoners of war. A thousand years ago and more, the temple steps had run with blood. The city's people had assembled where he stood to watch the gruesome rituals and join in feasts which—for the priests, at least—included human flesh. It would have been barbarous, and altogether fascinating.

Travis had his right foot on the lowest step before he caught himself. All thoughts of tampering aside, he was exhausted from the day's march and the week before it. If he started climbing now, he might collapse, fall down the steps and break a leg or worse. It could prove deadly if he was disabled, with no one but his guide and porters left to man the radio.

The climb could wait until the next day, when he'd had a good night's sleep. There would be time enough for him to stand atop the pyramid, beneath its solitary tree, and scan the site he had discovered.

He knew that was not entirely true, of course. The looters had been there before him, but they didn't count. "Discovery" had always been a term with flexible interpretations. He thought of Christopher Columbus and the New World, which was fully occupied when he "discovered" it for Spain, and started killing off the aborigines. Since thieves left no records, penned no articles for peer-reviewed journals, they had no claim on Site X beyond what they had stolen and sold to collectors abroad.

All that was finished now. If nothing else, Travis could force the government to recognize the city as a landmark. Soldiers would be sent to guard it, while surveyors took its measure and scientists were handpicked to explore its mysteries. Travis should be among them, based on his discovery and reputation, but he'd have to wait and see. There was as much backstabbing politics in archaeology as in the capital at Guatemala City or in Washington, D.C.

It pleased him to imagine the colleagues who had mocked his theories, silenced by his findings, even racked with envy. Let them suffer on an all-crow diet while he basked in adulation for a while.

He knew his moment in the spotlight would be brief. Site X would claim its fifteen seconds in the media, then slide back into darkness as new wonders vied and clamored for attention.

But for those few privileged to work the site, that sense of wonder might go on for years. If Travis could secure a posting to the team—not as its leader necessarily, but any job at all—he would be satisfied.

And if he couldn't, there was still a book to write, lectures to give, a few free meals and drinks in store for him when he returned from traipsing through the wilderness. Maybe it was a win-win situation, after all.

If only he—

A sudden gunshot snapped him from his reverie. His pistol, still securely holstered, was the only weapon that his team possessed.

Travis retreated from the north side of the pyramid, ran back around its corner, stopping when he had a clear view of the spot where he'd left his guide and porters.

A group of men in camouflage fatigues, all armed with military weapons, ranged along the tree line, watching him. His three companions stood with rifles pointed at their heads.

One of the jungle warriors raised a hand, clutching the pistol he had fired to summon Travis, and called out to him, "Come here, gringo. We must talk."

"BE CAREFUL WITH THOSE," the white man cautioned, as he slowly closed the gap between them. "We are not trespassing. I have papers granting us permission to be here. If you'd care to examine them—"

"Your name!" Alvarez snapped.

"I am Professor Howard Travis, sent from Princeton University to—"

"I will see your papers now."

The stupid gringo seemed to think they were official soldiers. Alvarez knew he could work with that, and keeping Travis off balance was a start. He watched as the man dropped his backpack, knelt before it, rummaging in one of its side pockets. Alvarez stood ready with his pistol, just in case the gringo's bumbling facade was trickery, a ploy to reach his holstered weapon or some other yet unseen.

"Be careful, gringo. Papers only."

"What? Oh, yes. Of course."

A moment later, Travis found what he was looking for and lurched upright, an old man's way of standing. Cautiously, watching the pistol Alvarez held pointed in his general direction, Travis crossed the open ground between them, holding out a plastic folder tied with twine.

"Remove the papers," Alvarez commanded.

Travis did as he was told, fumbling a little with the string because his hands were trembling. That alone told Alvarez that he was probably legitimate. An agent should have more control, although he might pretend to be afraid. At last, Travis removed a sheaf of documents, unfolded them and handed them to Alvarez.

He skimmed their contents, recognized the name of Guatemala's minister for preservation of antiquities, and reckoned that the papers were legitimate.

"What brings you here, Professor Travis?" Alvarez inquired, as if he didn't know.

"Exactly what you see around us," Travis answered, opening his arms in an expansive gesture as he half turned toward the ruins. "This site is a new discovery of great historical importance. It has never been—"

He stopped, and Alvarez could almost see the light bulb

levitating just above his head, a trick from old American cartoons. Frowning, the gringo dropped his arms and turned again toward Alvarez.

"How did *you* find it?" he inquired.

Alvarez raised his Browning Hi-Power pistol and squeezed its trigger, shattering the archaeologist's left knee. Travis collapsed, screaming, and writhed before him like a dying animal. He wasn't dying, though.

Not yet.

Alvarez knelt beside the wounded archaeologist and rapped him sharply on the forehead with the Browning's muzzle, hard enough to focus concentration without stunning him. He wanted Travis to experience the full scope of the pain without incessant wailing, so that Alvarez could finish with his questions. Gradually, by degrees, the gringo's eyes came into focus.

"You understand me, *sí?*"

"I…yes! For God's sake, what do you want?"

"The papers tell me only that you have been granted leave to wander through my country as you please," Alvarez said. "I must know *why* you've come. What brought you to this place?"

Travis seemed to have difficulty working out the problem in his mind, as waves of agony washed over him. At last, through gritted teeth, he said, "I came to save the site."

"Save it from what?"

"Looters. Despoilers." Yet another pause, before he added, "I'm on *your* side."

"I think not," Alvarez replied.

"But, you…you are…."

"We are not soldiers of the government that licensed your investigation," Alvarez admitted. "Quite the opposite, in fact."

"Rebels?"

"The last true Guatemalan patriots, in fact. Your country has subverted and corrupted nearly everything within our homeland. We will liberate it yet."

"I'm not political," Travis protested, grimacing as even the exertion of a simple sentence caused him pain.

"In these days, everything is politics," Alvarez said. "There is no history but what we make ourselves. No art but the decisive art of war."

"This place," the gringo gasped. "It means…so much."

"To you?" Alvarez sneered. "You never laid your eyes on it before today. Our sainted *presidente* doesn't even know that it exists. Given a choice, he'd burn this forest down and sell the land to Texas oilmen while the people starve."

"But you can stop that now," Travis protested. "With this site—"

"It *will* be stopped, gringo, but not by you. We need no advice from Princeton University or Washington on how to free our country from the death grip of her enemies."

"I mean no harm," Travis assured him, weeping now. Whether the pain or fear of death produced those tears, Alvarez couldn't say and didn't care. "I'll help you. We can save this place together. Never mind my leg. It's a misunderstanding. We can—"

"You are either truly arrogant, or else a simpleminded fool," Alvarez said. "In either case, I must reject your offer to help chart my homeland's destiny. We have done well enough without you, up to now, and so it will remain."

The color faded from the gringo's face. "You mean to kill me, then?"

"That may depend upon your answer to my question," Alvarez replied. "I ask again, who sent you here? How did you find this place?"

Incredibly, the wounded captive smiled. "Wouldn't you like to know?"

"I will know, gringo. You will answer me, if only with your dying breath."

Travis glanced at the bloody ruin of his knee, where both

hands clutched it. "I can't imagine anything hurts worse than this," he said.

"You are a fool," Alvarez said.

1

Driving west on Avenida la Reforma in a rented car, Mack Bolan reflected that Guatemala City seemed to be a city of museums. Before leaving the airport, he'd counted five large ones on his map of the capital's downtown district, a concentration of culture that rivaled Los Angeles and New York in density, if not in size and cost of the lavish facilities.

Ancient history was big business, as he'd recently learned. And bigger for some than for others. It had brought him here, some fifteen hundred miles from home, to do a dirty job that no one else would touch. Bolan had taken the assignment based on faith that he could handle it. And he would operate on that belief until somebody proved him wrong.

Rolling past the American Embassy on his left, Bolan was reminded that he was on foreign soil, a stranger to the area, its people and customs.

The man he'd come to see was a well-known player in the business that had made him rich at forty years of age.

Antiquities.

Bolan had never given them much thought before, but now he had a fair grasp of the market and the cash it generated every year. He knew that pre-Columbian items—those pieces predating the New World arrival of Christopher Columbus in 1492—could bring fabulous prices, depending on their age, size and condition. Even weathered or mutilated pieces might cost a small fortune, if their provenance was verified.

Not that collectors always gave a damn about the provenance. They always cared if the item was *real*, but many never stopped to ask if a specific article was stolen, either from its homeland or from some other enthusiast. Possession was nine-tenths of the law, and nerve sometimes made up the difference. Many collectors kept their treasures hidden from the world at large, enjoying them in private or with a small circle of trusted friends.

Bolan wasn't concerned with those collectors at the moment. He was looking toward a chat with one of their most affluent suppliers.

Santos Medina had a showroom in Zona 13, a quarter of Guatemala City that included the National Museum of Natural History and the National Museum of Archaeology and Ethnology. The showroom was open to walk-ins, though few of Guatemala City's residents or transient tourists could afford Medina's wares. His prices, if not astronomical, were high enough to keep the riffraff out and guarantee himself first rank among the nation's dealers in antiquities. His name was known in London, Paris, Amsterdam, New York—in fact, wherever serious collectors of pre-Columbian art could be found.

Medina's weakness, shared in common with his customers, was greed. He loved not only art and history, but the exorbitant income they could provide. And in pursuit of that sweet revenue, Medina had been drawn into black-market sales. His nine-to-five business in Guatemala City was legitimate, from all appearances, but he was also known to deal with looters on occasion and to sell their swag at hefty markups to his clientele abroad. Santos Medina was, in fact, a high-class fence.

How else could artifacts whose transportation outside Guatemala was a felony wind up in showcases throughout the world? Bolan wondered. There'd been a time, of course, when any self-styled archaeologist with pick and shovel could extract a fortune from the hinterlands of South America, Egypt or Southeast Asia, but those days were gone. Most nations now imposed stiff penalties for unlicensed removal of historic artifacts, including prison time and hefty fines.

That simply made the price higher on the items that were offered for sale.

Medina clearly had the fix in with particular authorities in Guatemala City who could strip him of his lifestyle and his freedom if they did their jobs according to the rules. He was at liberty, enjoying the high life, because corrupt officials always had their hands out for a payoff.

So, what else was new?

Corruption, great or trivial, no longer startled Bolan. He had seen too much of human nature in his time to be surprised by anything. At least the tomb raiders and traffickers in hot antiquities weren't killing anyone.

Or so he'd thought.

He turned north on Diagonal 12 and followed that highway to Zona 13, then turned left at the zoo. Medina's place of business was on a side street, relatively quiet and discreet. The whole block smelled of money, its boutiques and restaurants reminding Bolan of Rodeo Drive—minus the crass self-consciousness displayed by so many American celebrities and nouveau riche.

Bolan drove once around the block and found a place to park his rental car on the second pass. He left the car a half-block down from Medina's place and crossed the street, browsing at shop windows along the short walk back until he satisfied himself that he had not been tailed and there were no lookouts in place.

At least none who revealed themselves.

There was no reason, on the face of it, why Bolan's quarry should be guarded. The police would only take an interest in his trade if he stopped paying bribes, and his competitors were fellows like Medina, more accustomed to fine wines and fat cigars than cloak-and-dagger escapades.

Medina's showroom wasn't large, and certainly not garish.

Half a dozen pieces occupied a small display window in front, which would be covered with an armored screen after Medina closed for the night. Bolan surveyed the artifacts—crude figures, by his estimation, roughly carved and none revealing any trace of gold or other precious metals—and he had to wonder what the big deal was. Old figurines carved out of rock, none larger than his hand, displaying workmanship that might have been a child's.

But it was history, and from the price tags on display, Medina's customers had to be obsessed with owning relics of the past.

Bolan pushed through the glass front door into an air-conditioned room some fifteen feet across and twice that depth, extending to an office and a storage room in back. The only person visible was the proprietor himself, a portly man whose jet-black hair owed more to dye than nature. Gray hairs missed in the last treatment showed like flecks of dandruff in his thick mustache.

"Ola, señor," Medina said, emerging from behind the largest of his three showcases.

"You speak English?" Bolan asked him.

"But of course."

"Santos Medina, I presume?"

"The very same. How may I help you?"

"You can help yourself," Bolan replied. "Give me a reason why I shouldn't kill you where you stand."

2

The stranger's question took Santos Medina by surprise. His customers had asked him many things during his long career, including numerous requests for him to break this law or that, but none had ever challenged him to justify his own survival.

Thinking it a most peculiar joke, Medina forced a smile. "I do not understand, *señor*," he said, stalling. Meanwhile, his eyes took in the stranger—tall, athletic, clearly an American of serious demeanor.

"Let's break it down," the visitor suggested. "You're a man who deals with looters, thieves. You bribe police and politicians to ignore your crimes. You should've been in prison years ago, but here you are, living *la vida grande*. Do you think that's fair?"

"*Señor,* there must be some mistake. I—"

"Let me guess," the American interrupted him. "You're just a simple, ordinary businessman. You pay your taxes, love your wife, and wouldn't steal a peso if you found it lying on the street. How am I doing so far?"

Bristling, Medina answered, "It is true that I'm a businessman, although I've never married and I might indeed keep money if I found it unattended on the sidewalk. Who would not? As for your accusations that I am some kind of criminal, I must insist—"

"Hold on." The big man shifted slightly, drawing back the left side of his jacket to reveal a pistol nestled in a shoulder holster. "You're not in a position to insist on anything."

"Is this a robbery?"

"That's your line," the visitor said, "not mine. I'm here for information. If I get it, maybe you go back to business as usual. If not...."

He let the statement trail away, leaving Medina in no doubt as to his meaning. Cautiously, Medina answered, "Information?"

"That's the ticket. See, you're really not my primary concern. I'm not a cop. I don't care if you've got a bill of sale for artifacts you're moving overseas. Be clear on that. You're not under indictment."

"Sir, I assure you—"

"On the other hand, if I walk out of here unsatisfied, you don't walk out at all."

Medina didn't have to see the gun again. He had abandoned any hope that this was all some kind of tawdry joke, sponsored by one of his competitors in hopes of giving him a nasty turn. The man who stood before him was deadly serious.

Medina thought about the pistol he kept below his cash register. It was a hedge against robbery, and it had never been needed. Now, the six or seven paces separating Medina from the small nickel-plated weapon might as well have been a hundred miles. He knew that it would be impossible for him to reach the gun before the stranger cut him down.

And even then, his worst fear was that one shot might not finish him. That it might only be the start of something infinitely worse.

Medina swallowed hard. "While I admit no wrongdoing," he said, "if I may help you in some way and so dispense with this unpleasantness, by all means ask your questions."

"First, go lock the door and turn that sign around. You're closing for the day," the American said.

"That's most irregular, *señor*."

"I don't want anybody interrupting us," the stranger said. "Neither do you."

Medina nodded. "Very well."

He locked the showroom's door, peering outside as he did so, half hoping for a providential passerby whom he could signal with a glance to summon help. When none appeared, Medina turned the small sign dangling from a suction cup, showing the Closed side to the outer world.

When that was done, Bolan said, "Now show me the back rooms."

Medina felt a sudden lump in his throat and tried in vain to swallow it. The stranger meant to kill him. He was certain of it now. Why else go in the back, except for privacy in which to do the bloody deed?

"*Señor*, I've closed the shop as you demanded. May we speak here?"

"I don't want any late arrivals rapping on the door and nagging you to open up," the American said. "If we're not visible, they'll go away and try again tomorrow."

Fearing that he'd seen his last tomorrow as it was, Medina shrugged and led the man toward his office. As they passed the showcase with the large cash register, Medina once again considered lunging for his pistol. But he made no move in that direction, sensing that his best quick draw would not be good enough against this gringo with the pistol underneath his arm.

The stranger had a stone-cold killer's eyes, not burning with a crazy fire inside like some strange specimens he'd met, but all the more deadly for lacking emotion. The gringo might not kill him outright if Medina tried to reach his pistol, but there'd certainly be pain involved. And Medina feared that prospect almost as much as he feared death itself.

The office was immaculate, its tidiness a product of long habit and a trace of obsessive-compulsive behavior. There was a place for everything, and why should anything be found outside its place? It was a major reason why he'd never gone into the field to search for artifacts. That, and Medina's innate hatred for activities that made him break a sweat.

But he was sweating now.

If he survived this afternoon, Medina knew that he would have to throw away his shirt and underwear, perhaps the stylish suit itself. The air-conditioning was doing what it could to keep him cool, but fear bathed him in an oil sweat that made him feel unclean, repulsive, barely human.

"Here we are," Medina said, as boldly as he dared. "What is it that you wish to ask me?"

The intruder moved around his office for a moment, studying books and other items on the shelves, letting Medina stew in his own fear. It was a simple tactic, but effective. Standing there, confronted with a wall of stony silence, the antiquities purveyor felt himself begin to tremble. Silently, he prayed the stranger wouldn't notice.

"You have a nice place here," the gringo said at last. "It must cost plenty to maintain. I'm interested in the way you meet your overhead."

"*Señor?* I do not understand."

"Forget it. Let's just talk about the place they call Site X."

Santos Medina felt as though the man had reached inside his chest and squeezed his heart.

"THIS CAN'T BE right."

Antonio Ybarra stooped and squinted at the sign, as if proximity would change its message.

"What time is it?" he asked of anyone within earshot.

"Two-seventeen," Guillermo Obregon replied. "No, wait...it's two-eighteen."

Before Ybarra had a chance to snap at him, Ismael Rodriguez said, "It's not *siesta* yet."

"He never closes early," Ybarra said. Stepping closer to the door, he pressed his nose against the glass, hands raised on either side to screen the daylight from his eyes. "I don't see anyone inside."

Rodriguez shrugged. "So, something happened. Maybe he got sick. Or someone called. He had to go."

"And left the cash drawer open?" Ybarra asked. "I can see it, there."

"Maybe there wasn't time to shut it. If he's sick—"

Ybarra rose and rounded on them. "Who wants to tell Alejandro that we couldn't find him? You? Or you? I didn't think so."

Obregon looked vaguely ill himself, at the idea of failure and its consequence. "But if he's gone, what can we do?"

"I'm telling you, he wouldn't leave the cash drawer open if he wasn't in the store. Someone would have to drag him out of there at gunpoint and—"

His own words stopped Ybarra cold. Santos Medina was a businessman who worked on both sides of the law. There was a possibility that one of his illicit clients had dropped by, upset about division of the spoils or something else, and that the argument had turned to violence. Granted, he saw no body lying on the showroom's floor, but he could not see behind the three display cases, much less into the rear office or storeroom.

Now it was his turn to confront the possibility of failure and Alejandro's fury if he went back empty-handed and without an irrefutable excuse.

"We need to look inside," Ybarra said.

Obregon pressed his fingertips against the door, smudging the glass. "It's locked," he said.

"I know that, idiot!"

Ybarra slowly turned, surveyed the street and understood that he could not defeat the front door's lock without attracting unwanted notice. On a street like this, full of rich bastards, the police would definitely get a call and race to answer it. He and the others would be lucky if they survived the interrogations that could leave them broken men.

"There's a back door," he said, as dawning light broke through the haze of worry that enveloped him.

To Obregon, he said, "Go back and tell Arturo that he'll have to move the car. Just have him drive around until we meet him on the corner by the candy store. And come right back. You'll find us in the alley, or inside the shop."

"The alley. Yes," Obregon replied.

While Obregon moved north along the street to reach their vehicle, Arturo at the wheel and Jesús lounging at his side, Ybarra led Rodriguez in the opposite direction. Half a block beyond Medina's shop, they turned into a narrow alley and followed it until they met another running north to south behind the stores fronting the street.

The alley was wide enough for a garbage truck to pass through, collecting refuse from the cans and containers ranged along its length. Rich people must be different, Ybarra thought. Their garbage doesn't even smell the same.

He hated them for that, looked forward to the day when everything they treasured would be stripped away from them and given to the workers who had made it possible. It was a dream that nourished him and kept him going when it seemed that victory was still light-years beyond his grasp. Or that everything he'd done, the blood he'd spilled and tears he'd shed, had been in vain.

As they turned north again, Ybarra started counting doors. It wouldn't do for him to trespass on the wrong establishment. That would produce a call to the police and send him fleeing without having seen Medina, much less bringing home the information he'd been sent to fetch. A double failure certainly would not endear him to the boss, and if he was jailed…well, Alejandro might decide that it was risky leaving him alive in custody. Once that decision had been made, Ybarra was as good as dead.

Slow down! he warned himself. You haven't even tried the lock yet, and you're giving up already.

One of Ybarra's greatest faults was overthinking problems, picking them apart and studying all sides until his problem of the moment swelled to insurmountability. It was a self-defeating trait he had labored long and hard to overcome.

Without success.

He'd counted five doors, and there they were, behind Medina's store. They had the alley to themselves.

"Go on," Ybarra ordered, nodding at the door.

Rodriguez gently tried the knob. "It's locked."

Of course it was. Who but an idiot would leave his back door open to all comers, even in this ritzy neighborhood?

Ybarra reached into a pocket, palmed the set of simple lock picks that he carried with him everywhere. The last time he had used them, three weeks earlier, had been to crack the office of a right-wing tabloid after hours. Once inside, he and his men had trashed the place and left it burning.

That time was fun, but this move was dangerous.

"Keep watch," he ordered, as he knelt before the door with picks in hand.

"Hold on," Rodriguez whispered. "Suppose they're still inside?"

"Suppose who's still inside?"

"Whoever came to get Medina, like you said."

Ybarra hadn't thought of that. It made him want to slap himself.

"You have a weapon, yes?" he challenged.

There was a trace of hesitation as Rodriguez answered, "Yes."

"All right, then. We'll be quiet, take them by surprise and find out who they are. We'll get rid of them, and then tell Alejandro all about it."

"Like we're heroes, eh?" Rodriguez smiled, then let it slip, saying, "We should wait for Guillermo."

"While they waltz out through the front? We don't have time."

"But if they're gone already—"

"Then you have nothing to fear. Shut up and watch the alley. Let me work in peace!"

Rodriguez scowled but drew his pistol, holding it against

his leg as he stood guard, continuously scanning left and right along the alleyway. He may have been a nervous watchman, but Ybarra knew he was a crack shot with the automatic pistol in his hand and wouldn't hesitate to use it if required.

Ybarra concentrated on the door's stout lock. It taunted him at first, but he was patient and experienced. Around the ninety-second mark, the final tumbler clicked and settled into place.

Ybarra rose, returned the lock picks to their hideaway and drew his pistol. He clutched the weapon in his right hand, while his left closed on the doorknob, turned it and began to draw the shop's door slowly open, one inch at a time.

3

"Site X?" Santos Medina asked. "I'm afraid I don't know what you mean, *señor*."

"Maybe they didn't call it that," Mack Bolan replied. "The looters. Never mind. I want to hear about the latest batch of stolen artifacts you've been unloading in New York and London."

"Honestly, I don't—"

"It's funny," Bolan interrupted him. "When people start off saying 'honestly,' they're almost always lying."

"Please, *señor*—"

Bolan drew his Beretta, thumbed its hammer back and aimed it at a point between Santos Medina's eyes. "Let's cut the crap," he said. "Pretend your life depends on what you say, because it does. You deal in stolen artifacts. We both know that. I'm not a law-enforcement officer. I can't use your confession in a courtroom, even if I wanted to. I can, however, decorate this fancy office with your brains unless you tell me what I need to know. Right now."

A fresh stain marked the left leg of Medina's trousers. Bolan grimaced as the fence began to weep, then speak in fits and starts.

"Please understand," Medina whined, "I don't ask many questions."

"Just enough to make sure you're not dealing with the police, running some kind of sting," Bolan suggested.

"The police are not a problem, I assure you. My suppliers,

on the other hand…some of them can be dangerous. They are impulsive men, risk takers, sometimes barely civilized."

"The ones I'm interested in are civilized enough to be political," the Executioner replied.

"We don't discuss such things," Medina said. His answer had the ring of truth.

"But you'd be smart enough to check them out, regardless. Ask around and find out who they are, what they'll be doing with your money."

"One hears rumors," Medina said.

"One should share."

"My country is a land in turmoil. All my life there has been war of one kind or another. In the cities, in the countryside. The government pretends to have control, but there are groups that take a different view."

"And you agree with them?"

"I am a businessman, *señor*. I care nothing for politics beyond what helps me prosper."

"Now you're being honest. Spill the rest of it."

"A man brings artifacts that I can sell at a substantial profit, but the law insists that I must throw it all away, betray him to the government for robbing others who've been dead a thousand years." Medina frowned. "I take a dim view of such rules."

"And pay the cops to look the other way?"

"Donations are appreciated," Medina said. "Is it my fault that they barely earn a living wage?"

"So you're a philanthropist. I get it. Tell me more about these dangerous suppliers," Bolan said impatiently.

"Some eighteen months ago, two young men brought in a Mayan statuette. Pristine condition, solid gold. I naturally questioned them as to the source. They offered me a bargain, promised more—a great deal more—if I suppressed my curiosity. Under the circumstances, how could I resist?"

"But you still checked them out," Bolan replied.

"I posed some questions here and there," Medina said. "Discreetly. As you say, the young men were...political."

"And you've been moving product for them ever since?"

"They visit two, three times a month on average," Medina said. "Each time, they bring me items that are perfectly unique. I have no difficulty placing them with patrons of the arts."

Bolan lowered his gun but kept it ready in his hand.

"Smart money says you've tried to find out where their stash is located. Thinking you might eliminate the middleman."

"Why would I?" Medina asked. "They bring things to me. I don't go hunting in the field."

"But if you had to, in a pinch," Bolan replied, "I'm guessing you could manage. Say you got a tip from one of those impoverished cops. He calls and tells you that the government is cracking down on your political suppliers. Maybe there's no tip, but you turn on the radio and hear they've all been blown away. You wouldn't want to leave that kind of loot just sitting in the jungle. Right?"

"It would be sad and wasteful," Medina agreed.

"There you go. So you start snooping. All I need is everything you've learned, so far."

"Unfortunately for us both, I have not been successful in discovering their 'stash,' as you describe it. All my inquiries have been in vain."

Bolan raised the Beretta. "You're lying. You have one last chance to get it right."

Medina's shoulders slumped in grim defeat. His tears had dried, unlike his slacks. The dealer had resigned himself to loss, perhaps to death.

"Their trove is somewhere in the northeast, toward the frontier with Belize. That information cost me dearly, and it's all I have. If you must kill me, please do it quickly and be done with it. I have no more to tell you."

Staring over pistol sights, Bolan assessed his prisoner.

Medina's will was broken. He had given up all the information he possessed.

"All right," Bolan said. "If that's all you know, it's all you—"

Scuffling sounds from the adjacent corridor distracted him. Medina also tore his eyes away from Bolan's gun to glance in that direction, plainly startled by the sounds. He definitely hadn't been expecting reinforcements, and did not appear to be relieved.

Bolan stepped close enough to smell his prisoner, asking, "Who is it?"

"I don't know!" Medina answered. "Someone's come in through the back door, but it should have been locked."

"Employees?" the Executioner asked.

"No. My secretary is on holiday."

There'd been no noise of anyone jimmying the door. "Who else has keys?" Bolan demanded.

"No one."

Bolan pressed the Beretta's muzzle underneath Medina's chin, giving his head a backward tilt. "Don't make me ask you twice."

"No one! I swear it!"

Burglars, then? In broad daylight? Too much coincidence, Bolan thought.

Shuffling footsteps had nearly reached the office door. Bolan stood ready at Medina's side, as shadows fell across the threshold. First a hand with a pistol in it came around the door frame, followed by an anxious face atop a slender body. Close behind the first young man, a second followed, also armed.

The first man asked a question that eluded Bolan's grasp of Spanish, then he saw the gun in Bolan's fist and panicked, firing wildly. His companion followed suit, crouching and blazing off three rounds in rapid fire.

Bolan was airborne by that time, hurdling Medina's desk and dropping down behind it, just as bullets ripped into Medina's chest.

4

Washington, D.C., two days earlier

Bolan passed beside the Lincoln Memorial Reflecting Pool, scanning a line of soldiers ranged before him on his left. They had been turned to stone, as if afflicted with a Gorgon's glance, their bodies frozen in midstride. He noted that their helmets and their M-1 rifles were outdated, but the ponchos hanging to their knees would never change as long as army style remained utilitarian.

He counted nineteen fighting men, but some of them were only partly visible. The rear-guard soldiers were half buried in the earth, as if emerging from some private hell to face another enemy.

It was his second visit to the Korean War Veterans Memorial, and once again Bolan found the monument more moving—more human—than the wall of names dedicated to those killed in Vietnam. The Wall was overwhelming, with its nearly sixty thousand names inscribed on polished granite, cards and small bouquets scattered along its length. It was a hulking wedge of stone, blunt and impersonal. Bolan could see his face reflected in its polished surface, but he couldn't find the heart and soul of those who'd fought and died.

With the Korean monument, it was a different story. Life-sized soldiers were frozen at a moment in their lives none who'd managed to survive would ever forget. Their grim and haunted faces were familiar from his own wars. He could sympathize with their fatigue, their pain. As for the soldiers struggling endlessly to free themselves from clinging soil, he also understood the terminal frustration of pursuing wars that couldn't be won.

Wars that never ended.

Bolan had business on The Mall in Washington that afternoon. He'd been in the vicinity, doing a job in Baltimore, when Hal Brognola reached him on his sat phone and requested face time at his earliest convenience.

He knew there'd be a mission, hatched at Stony Man, for Bolan to consider. He was at liberty to turn it down, but rarely exercised that privilege. Brognola wouldn't call him if he didn't think it was important, something that required a dash of Bolan's special skills.

He left the petrified foot soldiers rooted in their tracks and continued on toward the Lincoln Monument. He had a hike ahead of him, but there was time and he enjoyed the sunshine on his face.

He watched the tourists as he made his way toward Honest Abe, imagining what it would feel like to exist full-time in their world, where the worst threats most of them would ever face were tardy bills or smudges on an X-ray. All of them would die, in time, but most would never know the panic-rage of mortal combat. The majority of them would never fire a shot in anger, would spill blood only by accident and then in minuscule amounts. Most didn't have an entourage of ghosts.

That was another reason Bolan led the life he'd chosen. Someone had to stand watch, keep the other members of the tribe both safe and relatively sane. Bolan could not protect them from themselves, wouldn't know how to try or where to start, but he could shield them from the predators.

Some of them, anyway.

A cloud had passed across the sun, shading the earth along

with Bolan's mood, but it was gone a moment later, passing into memory. His shadow also fell across the strangers who surrounded him, but none of them appeared to notice. They had no idea what he had done or risked on their behalf.

But then again, why should they?

It was a soldier's job to stand between the herd and those persistent predators that threatened its existence. Society had laws to curb their appetites, but predators by definition stood outside the fold, flouting the rules. When they could not be stopped by normal means, restrained by a traditional display of force, hunters like Bolan were assigned to weed them out.

Standing before the giant image of a President who'd saved the Union, liberating millions of enslaved Americans, Bolan wondered which predators he would be tracking this time. Where would they be found? What was their game?

"You come here often?" asked a gruff, familiar voice behind him.

Turning, Bolan looked at Hal Brognola. "Only when it's hunting season," he replied.

"Then you're in luck," Brognola said, as they shook hands. "I've got some rabid jackals that need thinning out."

"Tough job?" Bolan inquired.

"I couldn't rule it out."

"Travel?"

"Due south—and back in time."

"Don't tell me you've got a time machine."

"Not quite. Let's take a walk."

They circled Lincoln's monument, avoiding tourist clusters, speaking only loud enough to hear each other as they walked shoulder-to-shoulder.

"I don't guess you give much thought to ancient Mayans," the big Fed remarked.

"Not much," Bolan agreed.

"Remember anything about them from your old school days?"

A frown creased Bolan's face. "Nobody said we'd have a test today," he gibed. "Let's see. They came before the Aztecs and the Inca. Lived mostly in Central America, if memory serves. And most of them split without warning. Experts can't agree on when or why."

"A-plus," Brognola said. "I barely knew that much myself, before last week."

"Don't tell me you've got Mayans on the warpath," Bolan said.

"I wish. The bows and blowguns I could deal with. As it is, they're raising havoc from beyond the grave."

"I guess you'd better fill me in," Bolan remarked.

"About two years ago," Brognola said, "a lot of previously unknown Mayan artifacts began to surface in the States, in Canada and Western Europe. Experts clucked and scratched their heads. Nobody knew where they were coming from. Still don't for that matter. They sell for millions, and the source remains a mystery."

"Tomb raiders," Bolan said.

"No doubt. But since the items are uncataloged, it means they've tapped a previously undiscovered tomb—or several, from the volume that's been moving through the auction houses and museums."

"Sounds like a mystery for one of those museums to solve," Bolan replied.

"It would be, ordinarily," the man from Justice said. "But we've discovered a connection to the Guatemalan People's Liberation Front."

"I don't hear much about them anymore," Bolan said.

"They've been relatively quiet, but they're revving up again. Some bombings, rural executions, this and that. Feeling their oats. Ditching their vintage hardware for state-of-the-art."

"That costs money," Bolan said.

"Bingo. They used to rob banks, snatch some gringos for ransom, but the government cracked down on that, big-time.

We actually thought the movement had been crushed, but it seems they've reopened for business under new management."

"Financed by ancient artifacts?"

"At least in part," Brognola said. "One of their people came through Miami late last summer. He forgot to tell the customs guys about a ten-pound golden statue in his check-through luggage. When they found it, he went ape and tried to do a runner, managed to disarm a local cop before they put him down."

"So he isn't talking," Bolan said.

"Not unless we hold a séance," Brognola replied.

"I guess it couldn't be a one-time thing?" Bolan asked.

"That was my first thought, too, but we've been looking into it since then. The gist of what we've found suggests that either the GPLF stumbled on a major treasure trove, or else they're dealing with someone who has."

"That raises the ante from simple theft and smuggling to financing terrorism," Bolan said.

"Bingo, again."

"Does *anyone* have a fix on where the loot is coming from?"

"You mean besides the looters?" Brognola asked. "Not a clue, so far. The ivory tower crowd is calling it Site X, claiming it likely holds the key to understanding prehistoric civilization in the Western Hemisphere. I like the History Channel as well as the next guy, but I'm more concerned about bombs here and now."

"So, you want me to go and do what?" Bolan asked. "Spend a few weeks or months in the jungle, hoping I get lucky?"

"I can narrow it down a bit more than that," Brognola replied. "We've traced several of the international transactions to an antiquities dealer in Guatemala City. He probably won't have a fix on Site X, but he sure as hell knows who he buys from. Grab the chain and follow it—"

"Until I find the weakest link," Bolan finished the thought.

"That's it. And I have something for your viewing pleasure."

As he spoke, Brognola fished inside a jacket pocket, palming an object roughly the size of two cigarette packs taped together. It resembled a calculator, albeit with a larger screen and fewer buttons.

Bolan took it and looked it over. "Something new?"

"Call it a briefing in a box, with microchips. We've downloaded all the background information on the GPLF, present leaders we've identified, the dealer you'll be looking for when you arrive, plus any local color that seemed relevant."

"Okay."

"The catch is that you only get one run-through," Brognola continued. "Once you've viewed the file from start to finish, it erases automatically."

"No self-destruct?" Bolan asked.

"Sorry." Brognola chuckled.

"One other thing I'll need to know," Bolan said.

"Shoot."

"Who else is looking for Site X?"

"You mean, aside from every university on Earth that isn't strapped for cash and wants a king-sized feather in its cap? Maybe some private treasure hunters, though the government down there claims it's in full control."

"You can't guard what you haven't found," Bolan observed.

"So true. You should expect some competition, but it shouldn't be a traffic jam," Brognola said. "We're talking Guatemalan jungles, after all, not Central Park."

"The jungle may be safer than the park."

"Maybe. The way things stand today, I wouldn't want to bet my life on that."

Instead, Brognola thought, I'm betting yours. "What do you think?"

"About the job? Sounds doable," Bolan replied.

"So, you're in?"

"I'm in," the Executioner confirmed.

"If you need anything I haven't thought of—"

"Just a link in Guatemala City, for some hardware," Bolan answered.

"I slipped three into the briefing file, in case you need to shop around."

"That ought to do it."

"One more thing I have to mention," Brognola said. "It's about the sudden urgency. The Man's preoccupied with other situations, as you can imagine, but we've lost a man down there. Not one of ours, but an American."

"Who was he?" Bolan asked.

"An archaeology professor out of Princeton. Howard Travis. He was looking for Site X and wound up dead. The jungle doesn't leave much, but we know that he was shot repeatedly, most likely after torture."

"So, not natives, then."

Brognola shook his head. "Unless someone's supplying them with modern small arms."

"Where was he killed?"

"We only know where he was found," Brognola answered. "And that's just approximate. Northeastern Guatemala, midway between Flores and San Ignacio, which is the closest city in Belize."

"I don't suppose he had a map? X marks the spot?"

"No joy," the big Fed said. "He didn't even have a head. ID was made by DNA and the serial number on a surgical pin in his femur."

"Delightful."

"It's nature's way. Waste not, want not."

"So now it's payback time, because the prof went down?"

"You didn't hear me say that," Brognola replied. "But if you get a chance to level out the tab, why not?"

BOLAN CONSIDERED where it would be best to view the briefing presentation privately, without unwanted interruptions.

He decided on a large parking garage in Arlington and

drove around its dark, circling floors until he reached the roof. In his experience, few drivers chose the topmost level voluntarily, leaving their vehicles exposed to all the elements and doubling their travel time by stairs or elevator to ground level.

As expected, there was only one car on the rooftop when he got there. Bolan parked as far away from it as possible, in the northeastern corner of the lot. He cracked the rental's windows, to make sure that he would hear approaching footsteps if they came, and palmed the viewer Brognola had given him.

Settling for comfort in the driver's seat, Bolan thumbed Play. At first, the screen turned pearly gray, then it resolved into a stock news photo of guerrillas dressed in camouflage fatigues and ski masks, armed with a motley collection of rifles that included Russian AK-47s and American M-16s. A male voice Bolan didn't recognize began the briefing.

"Organized in 1989," it said, "the Guatemalan People's Liberation Front is a neo-Maoist movement drawing most of its membership from peasants in the rural countryside. Its reputed founders were Ernesto Guzman and Miguel Arroyo, two laborers on a plantation owned by Global Fruit. Both were arrested and presumably executed in the early part of 1991, by which time the GPLF had an estimated membership of two to three thousand."

As the voice addressed him, further still photos and clips of videotape filled the four-inch-square monitor screen. Guerrillas marched for Bolan, fired their mismatched weapons in a training exercise, and posed for group shots with their faces hidden. Next came rapid-fire still shots of offices and other buildings trashed by bombs or fire.

"The group pursued a campaign of attrition against Guatemala's government, while the junta responded in kind." Photos of bodies in the street and naked hooded prisoners flashed across the screen. "As incidents declined, it was assumed moves against the GPLF leadership had been successful. The group claimed no more acts of violence between

December 1998 and June 2001, when a sophisticated bomb damaged the Bank of America's office in Guatemala City."

"They've reopened for business under new management," Brognola had said. A wide-angle shot of the bombing gave way to a somber young face.

"According to current intelligence, Alejandro Cruz de Romero now commands the GPLF. He is twenty-three years old, a medical student who abandoned his internship in Guatemala City to pursue a life in revolutionary politics."

Like Che, Bolan thought, studying the face that filled the little screen.

"Cruz started with demonstrations on campus, facing academic probation after his first arrest for picketing a speech by the government's minister of health and human rights. Soon afterward, he quit school altogether and began writing articles for an outlawed leftist tabloid. An arrest warrant was issued for Cruz, but he escaped into the hinterlands. The bombing followed, and he issued claims of credit to the media."

Headlines rolled across the viewing screen. Alejandro Cruz had declared war on the regime that forbade him to speak peacefully. It was a story as old as human history, and dictators never seemed to learn from the mistakes of their predecessors.

"Since the resumption of hostilities," the faceless lecturer pressed on, "at least a thousand persons have been killed on both sides of the struggle for control in Guatemala. Some two-thirds of those are listed as subversives, either killed in battle by the army or detained and executed after trial. The rest are soldiers, government officials and high-profile hostages."

The story was familiar, following the pattern set by countless other "liberation fronts" over the past two hundred years. Bolan glanced up to scan the parking lot, then brought his eyes back to the viewing screen.

"While Cruz issues all of the group's communiqués and evidently plots its strategy," the neutral voice declared, "his second in command is thought to lead most operations in the field."

Another face appeared, this one daring to risk a narrow, crooked smile. The photo didn't have that mug shot quality. Instead, Bolan guessed it had been lifted from a snapshot taken by a friend, either before its subject joined the war or during one of those inevitable lulls in combat.

"Palmero Alvarez, known to his friends as Paco, serves as Cruz's chief lieutenant. Based on information from official files, they met while jailed for picketing and soon became good friends. Like Cruz, Alvarez comes from a relatively affluent background. He's college-educated, with a bachelor's degree in sociology, outspoken in his support of the urban poor and rural peasants. He was tried in absentia for the Bank of America bombing and sentenced to twelve years in prison. So far the army and police have had no luck arresting him. Subsequent trials have condemned both Alvarez and Cruz for murder and for crimes against the state."

Sentence them to death before they're caught and guarantee they won't surrender under any circumstances. Brilliant, Bolan thought.

The monitor screen cleared of faces, replaced by a succession of photos and slow pans depicting ancient artifacts. Some were relatively crude, hand-carved from stone, while others were elaborate and detailed, resplendent with gold, silver, jade and various gem stones. The finer work reminded Bolan of the loot from an Egyptian tomb, except that the carved faces had a distinctly Indian cast.

"Over the past two years," the voice stated, "numerous Mayan artifacts have found their way from Guatemala to museums and private collections throughout North America and Europe. None have been previously cataloged or registered, prompting experts from Harvard and Princeton to name the source Site X. So far, items from Site X have been traced to buyers in Los Angeles, San Francisco, Seattle, Chicago,

Cleveland, Dallas, Atlanta, Miami, Philadelphia and New York City. Outside of the United States, confirmed items have been found in Toronto, Montreal, London, Paris, Heidelberg, Geneva, and most recently in Moscow. Dating and marks equivalent to signatures on some of the more recent and expensive pieces verify a single source—wherever that may be."

I'm looking for fly speck in the jungle, Bolan thought.

"Total value of the pieces presently identified is estimated in the range of seven to eight hundred million U.S. dollars, retail. With expenses and allowances for markups after export, we assume the GPLF has cleared eighty to one hundred million dollars from illegal trade in Mayan artifacts. That income rivals the sale of conflict diamonds by guerrilla bands in Africa. It has provided Cruz and company with weapons and all manner of supplies, plus graft used to subvert employees of the ruling government. Disruption at the source will strike a telling blow against the GPLF and its leadership."

"Now all I have to do is find the source," Bolan said aloud.

As if in answer, another face appeared on the screen. This one was older, with bushy eyebrows and a matching mustache, hair swept back and held in place by gel or spray. It seemed to be another candid snapshot, taken in some kind of party atmosphere.

"Several trades," the voice said, "have been traced to this man, Santos Medina, a prominent art and antiquities dealer in Guatemala City."

Bolan memorized the addresses provided, deciding on the spot that he would try Medina's showroom first. Home visits meant a risk of meeting family, neighbors, too many civilians thrown into the mix. Facing the dealer at his home would be a last resort.

The briefing ended, as Brognola had promised, with names and addresses for three covert hardware dealers in Guatemala City. He memorized that information as well, then sat watching while the screen blurred into snow, as if a cable link had been disrupted. His briefing was complete and the file was gone beyond recall.

5

Guatemala City

Medina wasn't dead, but it would take major surgery to save him and the chances of a trauma team arriving in the next few minutes ranked well below nil. Bolan could hear him thrashing on the office floor, nearly within arm's reach beyond the desk, but hearing him and reaching him were two entirely different things.

Besides, he knew it would've been a wasted effort.

Medina had absorbed at least two hits to the chest cavity, and from the gurgling sounds he made trying to breathe, one of his lungs was punctured. Maybe both. He would be dead in minutes without speaking further, and the only thing he meant to Bolan now was one more obstacle between himself and freedom.

Crouching behind the desk, he listened to the two killers speaking quickly in Spanish, barely understanding one word out of ten in their dialect. It didn't take a linguist, though, to figure out that they were arguing about the best way to eliminate him, maybe guessing who he was and why he had been huddled with Medina when they burst upon the scene.

For Bolan's part, he wondered why they'd shot Medina. Had they come specifically to kill him, or had something that they'd overheard compelled them? Was the dealer hit by accident, perhaps, the clumsy shooters bungling a bid to rescue him from Bolan?

Whether they were incompetent or not, they had Bolan penned inside the office, pegging wild rounds at the desk where he sheltered. Neither of their weapons had a sound suppressor attached, and Bolan reckoned that the gunfire would attract a nosy neighbor soon. And on Calle Reynaldo that would mean speed-dialing the police for help.

He was running out of time, whichever way he sliced it. If he waited where he was, the shooters might get lucky, or the cops would show up and surround the place, preventing any of them from escaping. Bolan didn't fancy trying to explain his mission to the local law.

Bolan knew he had to blast out of the trap himself, and soon.

He had sixteen rounds in his Beretta, and he carried four spare magazines with fifteen each. The rub would be reloading under fire and on the move, if either of the gunmen had a clear shot at him on his journey to the door.

And he would have to pass them first.

Another bullet cracked the desk above his head, and Bolan had a sudden flash of inspiration. Craning to his left, he snagged Medina's wastebasket, which was filled with crumpled notes and wrapping paper. Bolan found his lighter, thumbed it to produce a flame and lit the wadded paper in the trash can. When it started smoking, Bolan rose to fire a shot across the desk, then lobbed the wastebasket through the office doorway to the corridor beyond.

It crashed against the far wall, startling his assailants into yelps of shock, then fell and spilled its blazing, smoking contents on the floor. It wasn't much, as conflagrations went, but Bolan only needed to distract his adversaries for a heartbeat.

He was up and moving toward the doorway even as the burning trash rebounded from the wall directly opposite and spread across the floor. One of the gunmen kicked the paper wads aside and stepped into the doorway with his pistol steadied in a good two-handed grip, already firing.

Bolan did the only thing that he could think of in that last split second, dropping low and slithering across the slick floor like a baseball player sliding into home. He took the impact on his left side, his right arm steady and extended with the sleek Beretta in his fist, hitting the shooter with a double-tap an inch above his solar plexus.

Stunning impact dropped the gunman where he stood, and Bolan's slide stopped short when his feet nudged the fallen shooter's ribs. Rising, he grabbed the young man's pistol and lunged through the office doorway in a diving shoulder roll, scattering wads and sheets of burning paper as he went.

Bolan found the second shooter crouched against the wall, wide-eyed and trembling. Nonetheless, his adversary didn't hesitate to fire a shot that passed within an inch of Bolan's face, a nearly lethal whisper in his ear.

Bolan returned fire with both pistols, two rounds each, and saw one shot go wide, drilling the plaster to his target's left. The other three tore into flesh and bone, bouncing the shooter off the wall and dropping him within a yard of Bolan, stunned and leaking crimson.

The Executioner kicked the shooter's pistol out of reach and crouched beside him. He could hear no sound of sirens yet, no clamoring outside the shop. He still had time. Not much, but possibly enough.

Raising the shooter's head and turning it until his eyes focused on Bolan's face, the warrior asked his name.

It came out almost as a gasp. "Ismael Rodriguez."

"Do you speak English, Ismael?"

"Yes. A little."

From the pallor of the young man's face, Bolan knew he was bleeding out internally. They didn't have much time.

"Who sent you here?" he asked. "Why did you shoot Medina?"

"He's shot? *Esta muerto?*"

Without a backward glance Bolan confirmed, "That's right. He's dead."

The dying shooter looked even more miserable, if that was possible. "Alejandro will be angry."

"Alejandro Cruz?"

"You know him?" Sudden hope flared in the young man's eyes. "Tell him it was an accident. We didn't mean to kill—"

Rodriguez stiffened in midsentence, then his eyes glazed over and he slumped into death. Rising, Bolan retreated toward the main showroom but stopped in the connecting doorway when he saw two men outside, their faces pressed against the glass.

Turning, he stepped around the second shooter's body and the bits of trash that barely smoldered now, moving along the corridor that had to have brought his would-be killers to the office. At the rear, he found a door standing ajar and pushed it open, standing with two pistols at the ready while a broad slice of the outer alley was revealed.

All clear, as far as he could see.

Bolan stepped through and shut the door behind him, tucked the liberated pistol underneath his belt, in the small of his back. He was about to holster the Beretta when a man called out from Bolan's left, "Hey, gringo! Stop!"

GUILLERMO OBREGON HATED to play the role of errand boy. It galled him but he found himself outranked, and when Antonio Ybarra had sent him with a message for the others in the car, he had no choice but to obey.

He'd found Arturo and Jesús in a small parking lot, a long block from Medina's showroom, and delivered Ybarra's message. They had to move the car, circle the block until they saw the others waiting on the corner near the candy store, three blocks due south.

"What's happening?" Arturo asked, speaking around the stub of a cigar.

Ybarra had said nothing about keeping it a secret. "The

shop's closed when it shouldn't be," Obregon replied. "We're going in the back way."

"We?" Jesús chimed in. "Who's we?"

"Antonio, Ismael and me."

"You'd better run on back, then," Arturo said, almost sneering. "They could be inside by now. Maybe they need your help."

Jesús snickered at that, a wheezy mocking sound. Obregon longed to reach inside the car and slap his face, but he had more important business at the moment.

"Shall I tell Tonio you found his orders humorous?"

Arturo and Jesús stopped laughing, their hilarity replaced by sour faces. "I do what I'm told," Arturo said, and twisted the ignition key to prove his point, revving the engine into life.

"So do we all," Obregon said.

He turned away, stepped clear to let Arturo pull out of his parking space, and watched as the sedan rolled toward the street. More laughter rippled from the car as it retreated, leaving Obregon with cheeks aflame and fists clenched at his sides.

He scowled after the car, considering a rude gesture, but Alejandro always warned against attracting notice in a public place. He reckoned Antonio Ybarra should remember that, before he started breaking into stores on Calle Reynaldo, but that call did not belong to Obregon. He was a soldier and had to follow orders, even when he thought they smacked of madness.

As he walked back toward Medina's showroom, with the car already lost to sight, Obregon wondered why the five men had been dispatched for a simple meeting with the antiquities dealer. There had been no problems that he was aware of, but his rank precluded Obregon from being privy to the higher-level inner workings of the group. He hoped to change that situation by observing all the rules, obeying every order without question, but he feared that Antonio and others might be prejudiced against him in their hearts.

The way they teased and laughed at him sometimes infuriated Obregon, but he could not afford to let it show. Displays of temper would not help him win promotion, and the merest hint of insubordination toward superiors could get him drummed out of the GPLF's ranks.

Or worse.

The Guatemalan People's Liberation Front had no retirement plan, no severance package for disgruntled former members. A person who left the group or was expelled immediately posed a threat to every other member. Execution was the remedy, as Obregon himself had seen on two occasions since he took his oath of loyalty. In one case he had been a member of the firing squad, a means of blooding him for combat later on.

Still, if and when he had the chance to safely be avenged against his tormentors…

He spied a narrow alley north of Medina's shop and turned into it as if that had been his destination all along. It led him to a wider alley set behind the shops, where trash collections could be carried on without offending any of the shoppers. Obregon despised those wealthy parasites, hoping that he would live to see the day when all of them were dispossessed. But first, he had a job to do.

He looked in vain for Antonio and Ismael, but the alley offered him no clues. Downrange, a well-dressed gringo stepped into the alley through the back door of a shop. It seemed more than a trifle odd, his curiosity dissolving into panic as Obregon counted doors and realized the man had been inside Medina's store.

Ybarra and Rodriguez wouldn't let him go, at least without some questions asked. And that could only mean—

Obregon drew his pistol, clumsily, and shouted down the alleyway, "Hey, gringo, stop!"

6

Bolan made the distance eighty feet or more. Not optimal for dueling with a semiautomatic pistol, but he'd made less likely shots. Turning to face the stranger, Bolan leveled his Beretta, then recoiled from two incoming shots in rapid fire. One bullet sizzled past his left cheek, while the other struck the wall to his right and stung his neck with concrete chips.

Bolan ducked and ran, fired almost aimlessly, and saw his adversary stumble. Even as he thought it had to have been a very lucky shot indeed, the stranger found his footing and squeezed off another running shot. This one was farther from its mark but close enough to keep Bolan in motion, racing toward the nearest intersecting alley that served Calle Reynaldo.

Safety in numbers was an overrated concept. Bolan was a stranger in this city—worse, a gringo—and he knew he could expect no aid from anyone along the street beyond a phone call to the law. Likewise, there was no guarantee that his pursuer would desist from shooting in the presence of civilian witnesses. Some reckless shooters didn't care, while some enjoyed performing for an audience. A handful wouldn't have it any other way.

Bolan would have to deal with his pursuer, and soon, before their footrace turned into a massacre of innocents. The alley he sought was forty feet ahead, and it was thirty feet from there to reach the street. His car was parked another half-block south, but reaching it could be a problem. Reaching it unnoticed by prospective witnesses would be even harder.

Ducking another bullet, Bolan knew that his pursuer wasn't a policeman in plain clothes. There'd been no warning cry of *"Policia!"* to demand submission, and he didn't think a detective would be working the alleys—even one as relatively upscale as his present battleground.

That posed another problem for the Executioner, since it could only mean the two men he'd disposed of in Medina's shop were not alone. And if three had been dispatched to see the dealer, why not four or more? Where was their vehicle, if three had come on foot to the back door? And why was number three so late?

Because the others sent him somewhere with a message, Bolan figured. It could've been a phone call, but he guessed that Guatemala's urban rebels had to have cell phones. That meant a face-to-face with someone else nearby, potential reinforcements or a closing trap.

The alley's mouth opened on his left. Bolan slid into it, considered pausing for an ambush, then decided not to waste his narrow lead. Instead of crouching in a narrow passage where he had no cover, hoping that his adversary wouldn't score a lucky hit before he fell, Bolan poured on the steam and ran for daylight, sprinting for the street ahead.

Behind him, shooter number three was keeping pace. After his early stumble, he had shown resilience and a decent nerve. Bolan respected that, but it would not restrain him if he found an opening to drop his enemy.

As if in answer to that silent thought, he heard running footsteps behind him. A command called out in Spanish this time, followed by another pistol shot. The slug flew past him, across the street, drilled the window of a small bridal boutique and struck a mannequin attired in wedding finery.

Bolan spun in midstride, fired a quick double-tap, then resumed his headlong sprint. He didn't wait to see if either of his shots had found the mark, but from the scuffling, gasping sounds behind him he presumed a hit. Slowing a bit as he approached the open sidewalk, Bolan stowed his piece and made a point of not colliding with pedestrians. Glancing both ways without a break in stride, he lunged into the street.

A woman's squeal behind him told Bolan that his pursuer hadn't given up the chase. He couldn't stop to watch the other man with traffic rushing toward him, car horns blaring their annoyance, but he had a mental image of the scene. A lurching figure on unsteady legs, perhaps a splash of crimson on his shirt, waving his pistol as he tried for a clean shot.

Bolan zigzagged through traffic, putting cars between himself and the shooter whenever possible. He spotted his own vehicle, less than a hundred feet away, but even if he reached it someone on the street was bound to note his license number, offer it to the police.

Another woman's scream was matched by screeching brakes and squealing rubber, muffling a heavy sound of impact. Bolan reached the other sidewalk, turned in time to see his adversary sprawled across the hood of a sedan with two men seated in the front. The body surrendered to gravity and slid off the near-side fender as he watched.

The driver should've been in shock, emerging to behold the man he'd struck, but he was staring after Bolan, saying something to his passenger. Now both men had a fix on Bolan, hatred mingled with surprise on both their faces. Bolan saw the driver twist his steering wheel, crushing the fallen shooter's legs and swerving into northbound traffic as he came for Bolan in a rush.

There was no time to reach his rental now and make a car chase of it. All he had time to do was run.

THE FIRST JOLT of his wheels crushing Guillermo's flesh and bones sickened Arturo Machado, but he steeled himself against the feeling and accelerated toward the man who was responsible for all of it.

Guillermo had been following a gringo when he lurched into the path of their approaching car, splashing his blood across the hood and windshield as he died. Already wounded, from the look of him, pistol in hand, and he was all alone in the pursuit. Where were Ybarra and Rodriguez? Why was Machado suddenly left to make the decisions himself?

No matter.

It was time to act, and Machado had always been better at *doing* than *thinking*. He wasn't a planner and rarely thought past the next hour unless he was pressured to do so. Machado knew that he would never be a strategist, rising high in the ranks of the movement, but he enjoyed the struggle for its own sake.

For the moment, though, Machado's only goal was to destroy the gringo who had made him kill Guillermo, and perhaps had killed his other friends as well.

Jesús yelped at him to watch the traffic, but Machado let the other motorists watch out for *him*. They didn't know who they were dealing with, but any one of them could soon find out if they obstructed him or tried to interfere with his revenge. The next body thumping beneath his wheels would be the gringo bastard, screaming as he died, and then—

Just as the runner ducked into another alley ahead, Machado had an unaccustomed flash of insight. He should try to take the man alive, if possible. He'd deliver him to Cruz and Alvarez for questioning. That kind of foresight—not to mention courage—just might move him up the GPLF's ladder after all.

"He went in there!" Jesús directed.

"I'm not blind," Machado answered, swerving sharply toward the alley's mouth. A woman and her child leaped back in time to save themselves, their wide eyes gaping at Machado as he passed.

The narrow alley closed around them, barely wide enough for the sedan. Machado recognized his error instantly and mouthed a bitter curse. The runner was in front of them, all right, but in the claustrophobic confines of the alley they could only chase him, couldn't open either door enough to step out of the car or even risk a wild shot from a window without slamming face and skull into a wall on either side. If they could overtake the gringo, run him down, they'd still be forced to pull out of the alley and walk back to fetch his body.

"Damn it!"

"What?" Jesús asked.

"Never mind. Just watch him!"

"I'm already watching him."

"Well, keep your eyes—"

In front of them, the gringo did a kind of running pirouette, firing his pistol on the spin before he turned his back to them once more and ran for daylight at the alley's mouth. Machado didn't count the shots. He was too busy ducking as two bullets pierced the windshield and at least one more spanged off the roof of the sedan.

It took only a heartbeat of distraction. When Machado ducked, they drifted slightly to the left. It would have been a trifle on the open road, but in the alley it produced a monstrous gating sound as paint was flayed from the driver's side, scarring the steel underneath. Machado jerked the wheel to correct his course and went too far to starboard, grinding the passenger's side down to match.

Jesús, meanwhile, had managed to return fire by the only means available, directly through their punctured windshield. Three shots from his pistol echoed in the car, numbing Machado's ears, before Machado struck him with a jarring backhand blow.

"Don't kill him, for God's sake!" he ordered. "I want him alive!"

"But, Arturo—"

"Just do as you're told!"

Jesús was even less of an accomplished thinker than Machado. By the time he got around to challenging Machado's authority, they should have their quarry in the bag. Machado would explain it to him then, in such a way that Jesús would be forced to marvel at his brilliance.

The alley ended thirty feet in front of them, cars and pedestrians visible, passing back and forth unaware their city had become a war zone. They would find out soon enough, but in the brief time that remained, Machado desperately sought a plan to save himself.

He didn't mind hitting pedestrians. His vehicle would crush them flat. But slamming into other cars, perhaps even a bus or truck, would definitely crimp Machado's plans. He didn't want to die, much less be captured by police and hauled off to the nightmare rooms of their interrogation center. Braking would give the gringo runner an advantage, but exploding from the alley at full speed could be Machado's last mistake on Earth.

There was no time to think about it. He was running out of time and space. Machado stomped down on his brake, clutching the steering wheel with all his strength, and hung on as they skidded toward the alley's mouth.

BOLAN TURNED LEFT as he cleared the alley, pressed his back against the wall of what appeared to be a stylish hair salon, and waited there with the Beretta in his hand. He heard the chase car's engine revving, then a squeal of brakes, the sliding sound of tires on pavement as if some great beast was dragging its unwieldy carcass over gravel.

Bolan wondered if the driver had been quick enough in braking, and he had his answer in a heartbeat, as the battle-scarred sedan slid halfway from the alley's mouth, stopping a yard or less before its grille would have collided with a passing taxicab. The driver, seen in profile, had a vaguely dazed expression on his face.

"Not bad," Bolan remarked, and shot the driver through his forehead as he turned to place the voice. Crimson exploded from his head in back, spraying the passenger, the dashboard, the seats.

Bolan was leaning down to get a clear shot at the shotgun rider when a muzzle-flash erupted from the car's interior. He heard the bullet pass him, like a tiny supersonic aircraft, and he ducked before another shot flew overhead.

Women were screaming on the sidewalk now, men shouting and dragging their loved ones to cover where it could be found. Bolan was also seeking cover for himself, the more so as he heard sirens approaching. At the moment, though, the best that he could do was to crouch beside the chase car, close enough to keep the passenger from glimpsing him.

And then the car began to move.

The lifeless driver's foot had slipped from the brake, perhaps nudged the accelerator in the process. Either way, the flayed sedan rolled forward into traffic, just in time to meet a hulking garbage truck. The impact spun it back onto the sidewalk, clipped a fire hydrant and sent a frothy geyser shooting skyward.

Bolan edged back toward the alley that had been his runway moments earlier. The crash had managed to distract any witnesses, and he did not intend to waste the opportunity that had been granted him. Leaving the crumpled chase car and its sole survivor to the law, he holstered his Beretta, turned and ran back toward Calle Reynaldo and his waiting vehicle.

The sirens had drawn closer, but the sound of them told Bolan that they still had several blocks to travel. Halfway down the alley, he began to think what might be waiting for him at the other end.

No shooters, he was fairly sure of that. There had been witnesses, of course, but his experience told Bolan that they would be clustered near the fallen shooter's body, soaking up the death experience before the uniforms arrived to spoil their morbid fun. If he was cool about it, didn't draw undue attention to himself, there was a decent chance that he could reach his car and drive away unnoticed.

Or at least without some hawk-eyed citizen remembering his rental's license plate.

The gringo thing was one big strike against him, but at least he could reduce the odds of being recognized. Eyewitnesses in crisis situations rarely got the details right, and Bolan reckoned he could run a con job if he had to.

Stripping off his jacket, he removed the shoulder holster next and wrapped it in the jacket, which he draped across his arm. He took a pair of sunglasses from his jacket pocket, put them on and ran his fingers through his hair.

Emerging from the alley with an easy stride, Bolan performed a fair impersonation of a tourist. He showed interest in the clutch of gawkers gathered in the middle of the street, obstructing traffic, but he didn't join them. Lingering just long enough to make it all seem natural—and reassure himself that no one on the nearby sidewalk seemed to notice him—he turned away and walked toward his rented car.

The worst part was unlocking it, settling into the driver's seat and fastening his seat belt. That was the moment when—at least in Hollywood productions—gunmen or police would suddenly surround him, cutting off all access to escape.

But nothing happened.

Bolan turned the key, started his car without a hitch and pulled away from the curb into the right-turn-only lane. He followed all the signs and arrows, turning one block short of where his former enemy lay stretched out on the pavement, putting the scene behind him just as flashing lights came into view, approaching from the north.

It had been too damned close for comfort, but he never second-guessed the blessing of survival. Bolan hadn't managed to obtain the information he'd been hoping for, but at least he had a pointer in the general direction of his quest. It wasn't much, but it was *something*, and he'd ruined something for his adversaries in the process.

They would need another dealer. Santos Medina was out

of business and his tomb-raiding suppliers would be forced to shop around. It might not put a crimp in their activities for long, but again, it was at least a small accomplishment.

The next phase of his search would mean leaving the city streets behind and entering a different kind of jungle, one with which the Executioner was perfectly familiar.

It would almost be like going home.

To Hell.

7

Alejandro Cruz wanted to punch someone, release his anger in a screaming, kicking frenzy, but he didn't dare. The news had come from Guatemala City, far away. He couldn't reach the messenger and any wild display in camp would only make the men question his sanity. That, in turn, could lead to desertions, and Cruz needed every man he had.

But it was bitter news indeed. If not the worst, then bad enough to serve until complete disaster came along.

The satellite-phone message had been terse, abbreviated to prevent state security from tracing the call to its source. Santos Medina was dead, along with four of Cruz's men. A fifth was still unconscious in the hospital, after some kind of accident, and Cruz had passed the word to silence him for good.

He couldn't have one of his soldiers spilling everything he knew—whatever that might be—simply because the fellow wished to spare himself a little pain. Better to still his tongue forever than to take a risk of losing more men, maybe losing everything.

Cruz had already lost enough.

He'd sent the men to quiz Medina, maybe threaten him if it was necessary, but Cruz never meant for anyone to kill the dealer. Granted, there were indications that Medina had been skimming off the top, discounting sales figures before they were reported and the cash delivered, but that was a business matter. Cruz was willing to negotiate a settlement, express his personal displeasure to Medina by nonlethal means, but now that opportunity had been snatched from his hands.

Cruz felt the incandescent anger in his face, burning beneath his swarthy skin. It might not show, but anyone who knew him would pick up on his explosive mood and give him a wide berth until the rage subsided.

And the worry. There was always that.

Because Medina had not killed his men. That much was obvious. The dealer was a soft man. He would argue, wheedle, but he didn't have that kind of violence in him. Certainly he did not have the skill or courage to kill four of Cruz's men and send a fifth one to intensive care.

An accident, his caller had reported for the fifth man, without giving any details, but Medina and the others had been shot. Cruz had confirmed that much by tuning in to a midday news broadcast that issued from the capital. Police had no suspects in custody, but smuggling was suspected as a motive. No names but Medina's had been aired so far, pending reports to next of kin.

Good luck with that, Cruz thought.

His men had been indoctrinated not to carry any personal identification, and none of those he'd sent to see Medina had ever been fingerprinted. He would have been surprised if one in five had ever seen a dentist, so there'd be no records to examine, no X-rays or charts to help identify the dead. Once his assassins reached the survivor and silenced him, there would be no trail back to Cruz.

And yet the mystery remained. Who killed Medina?

If it was his own men, why would they exceed their orders, knowing Cruz would have them flayed alive? And who killed them, after the dealer died?

The radio broadcast told Cruz there had been shooting and a foot chase, followed by a car crash that sent two men to the hospital. He didn't care about the truck driver, whose broken

legs would heal in time and who knew nothing of the incident
beyond his tiny part. One of his men was comatose, a poor prospect for liberation from the doctors, and would soon be dead.

But that left one or more persons at large who knew the
reason for Medina's death and the resultant hardship Cruz
would suffer for it.

That was the real tragedy and reason for his anger. Alejandro Cruz cared nothing for the six lives wasted, only for their
meaning to the movement. And Medina's death would cost
the movement dearly.

Cruz would have to find another dealer, or give up on the
single greatest source of income that the Guatemalan People's
Liberation Front had ever found. Sufficient treasure still remained to help Cruz and his warriors win their struggle, but
he couldn't hawk it on the streets of Guatemala City. Cruz had
no contacts of any value in the world where ancient artifacts
brought prices that were both obscene and irresistible. He
might've broken down the larger, richer pieces, sold them for
their weight in gold and gems, but that would be a shameful
waste for all concerned.

He needed help, and that meant searching for another middleman to move the goods. He would need someone greedy
and corrupt enough to do the job—not a problem, sadly, in
his homeland—and someone whose fear of Cruz and the
GPLF would keep his avarice within acceptable parameters.

Cruz was a revolutionary, but he wouldn't ask a businessman to work free of charge. He knew enough of human nature to believe that greed often did more to motivate a man or
woman than commitment to a holy cause, while fear alone
might lead to acts of desperation.

He needed someone like Medina, who would sell his soul
for a percentage of the treasure without overstepping the
terms of their agreement. Once he found a candidate, negotiations could begin. Medina's death would likely raise the
cost of doing business, but he was prepared to live with that.

There was too much at stake for Cruz to simply walk away. He'd never have another chance like this again, and without it there was a good chance his cause would fail.

But selling off the treasure wasn't Cruz's only problem. Someone had found Medina, killed him at the very moment when Cruz planned to question him about the irregularities in their arrangement. That suggested their secret was exposed—and if the dealer had been compromised, why not the hoard itself? Before he thought about finding another dealer, Cruz had to protect the vast reserve of wealth that still remained. If it was taken out from underneath his very nose, snatched from his fingertips, then all was lost.

He palmed the sat phone, keyed a number, and heard a gruff voice answer on the second ring. "We need to talk," Cruz said. "Come see me. Now."

TOMAS AGUIRRE KNEW the sentries were in place before he stepped out of his powerboat onto the muddy riverbank. He knew it, but they still surprised him with the suddenness of their appearance from the undergrowth and shadows. One moment, he and his pilot shared the river with a flight of raucous birds; the next, four wiry men with automatic rifles had him covered, treating him as if they'd never played this game before.

In fact, Aguirre couldn't swear they had. He didn't recognize their solemn faces, paid so little heed to his escorts between one visit and another that he didn't know if these men had been sent to greet him previously or if they were new. Cruz had a high attrition rate among his soldiers, losing men and adding new ones all the time. Aguirre sometimes wondered where Cruz found fresh sacrificial lambs, but warfare wasn't his concern except where it impinged upon his business.

Ancient treasure fired Aguirre's soul, both for its beauty and the money it could bring into his hands. He had a reputation among those who hunted pre-Columbian artifacts throughout Central and South America. At one time or another, Aguirre had cracked the tombs of Aztecs, Incas, Mayans and Toltecs, sharing their wealth with the world.

And keeping some for himself, of course.

Some dusty academic might run off and risk his life for science, even for the thrill of being mentioned in some stuffy academic journal, but Tomas Aguirre couldn't eat or drink footnotes. He couldn't live on praise alone. An honorary college degree couldn't keep him warm at night.

Aguirre loved the hunt, of course, but he also demanded a reward for his exertions. In a perfect world he might have done the same thing purely out of love for the adventure, but he wasn't living in a perfect world.

Far from it, as the riflemen reminded him.

Aguirre left his pilot with the boat, one of the gunmen staying with him. The others led Aguirre through the rain forest toward Cruz's camp. He never found it in the same place twice, though Cruz always pitched camp in the same general area, staking his claim to a range of some two hundred square miles. The mountains, farther inland, were for dire emergencies when Cruz and company were forced to disappear completely for a time.

That hadn't happened recently, but from the tone of Cruz's voice when they had spoken on the sat phone, anything was possible.

They reached the camp ten minutes after passing from the riverbank into the forest. First, Aguirre smelled the cooking fires, and then he heard the sounds that accompany day-to-day human activity. Men talking, chopping brush or wood, digging latrines—or graves—repairing their machines. A moment after that, they cleared the last checkpoint and his escorts led him to where Cruz sat outside an old familiar tent.

"You're late," Cruz said without preamble.

"No, I'm not," Aguirre said. "I left within five minutes of your call. I traveled in a river launch, not in a time machine."

For just a moment there, Aguirre thought that he had pushed his luck too far. Cruz glared at him, tight-lipped, then shrugged off some of what was eating at him, waving one hand toward a canvas camp seat near his own.

Aguirre sat and asked the rebel chief, "What's wrong?"

"Medina's dead," Cruz told him, cutting to the heart of it.

Aguirre didn't have to feign dismay. "For God's sake, when? What happened?"

"Just this afternoon," Cruz said. "I told you he was stealing from us."

"So you *killed* him? Alejandro, why on Earth—"

"It wasn't me," Cruz said. "At least, I don't believe so."

"I don't understand you."

"I sent men to speak with him, but just to speak." Cruz frowned and shrugged again. "Maybe to frighten him a little, if they had to. You know how these things are done, Tomas."

"All right. What happened?"

"All of them are dead now," Cruz replied. "There was someone else, then shooting and a car crash. I'm still looking into it. We should know more soon." Cruz fanned the air as if dispersing flies. "That isn't why I called you here."

"It's not?"

Aguirre was surprised again. Medina's death was serious enough to rate a summons, since it spelled potential doom for his relationship with Cruz and all their dreams of profit in the future. If the rebel leader had a worse problem to share, Aguirre wasn't sure he cared to hear it.

"We'll find another dealer somewhere," Cruz assured him. "It may take some time, but greedy men are all around us. That is not what troubles me."

Aguirre saw it then, before Cruz could complete his thought. "The treasure," he replied.

Cruz nodded. "If the men who killed my soldiers know about Medina, they may soon discover where the artifacts came from. Perhaps they know already and—"

"It's not that simple," Aguirre said, interrupting Cruz. "It took me half a year to find the place, and I was working from a map of sorts. They can't just ask the tourist office for directions and drop in to loot the place."

"You worked with guides, diggers, porters. We're not the only two men on the planet who know where the treasure lies."

Aguirre grimaced. "We'll have to move it all," he said. "As soon as possible."

Cruz nodded. "That is why I called you. We should start today, right now. It may already be too late, but if we catch the bastards stealing from us we can leave them there."

"I have only a dozen men," Aguirre said. "They'll need time to break camp and—"

"Never mind your men," Cruz said. "Use mine. This camp is closer to the site than yours. It saves you time. I'll have nearly a hundred men, when Paco gets back from patrol. We should hear from him soon."

"I hope you're right," Aguirre said, "for all our sakes."

8

The riverboat could take him only so far. Bolan had picked his guide on instinct, judging by the scars that he could see and by the attitude that told him he had found a river rat who didn't knuckle under to authority. The state police could doubtless find some way to make him talk, but that would only happen if they had some reason to suspect him of wrongdoing.

And for Bolan's part, he didn't plan to leave any clues behind.

His gear was packed, his weapons more or less concealed to give the river pilot a degree of plausible deniability. They both knew that the scar-faced pilot didn't buy his cover as a census taker for the Global Wildlife Fund, but all the pilot really needed to know about Bolan was that he'd paid in full with cash, up front.

They hadn't talked about a pickup, made no rendezvous appointment for the end of Bolan's sojourn in the wild. The Executioner had no idea how long his search would take, where it would lead him, or if he would manage to come out alive. He carried one week's worth of rations in his pack, and if that didn't last him he would have to try his skill at living off the land.

It was among the first things that he'd learned in Special Forces training and he put that training into practice many times, from Southeast Asia to the Congo basin, the Caribbean and South America. He'd learned the tricks, remembered all of them—and knew they wouldn't mean a damned thing to him if he let some unseen sniper have a lucky shot.

The river pilot operated from a jetty on the outskirts of Flores, the last town in northeastern Guatemala that appeared on Bolan's map. There would be others in the jungle—trading posts and missions, scattered native villages—but Bolan hoped to bypass all of them unless some pressing need compelled him to seek contact with humanity.

The settlement he sought had been abandoned for a thousand years or more. The land would have reclaimed it, for the most part, helping to conceal its secrets from the eyes of man. If not for stubborn human perseverance or a bit of pure dumb luck, it would still have been forgotten and ignored, as it had been for bygone centuries.

But someone had discovered it, had tunneled through the ferns and creepers to reveal its precious secrets. Site X was suddenly a problem in the present tense, and Bolan had been sent to deal with it.

But how?

His stash of gear included C-4 plastique, but he couldn't haul enough explosives on his back to vaporize a city carved from stone. In fact, Bolan had no idea what he would do when he found the ancient site.

Assuming that he *could* find it.

There was a decent possibility that he would strike out all around, roam aimlessly through brooding jungles without ever coming close to his intended target. If that happened, he would have to set himself an arbitrary time limit, a cutoff point from which there was no deviation based on personal embarrassment at failure.

If he couldn't find the city and he wouldn't leave until his mission was completed, he would die.

It was just that simple.

Bolan was prepared to sacrifice his life each time he took a job, but it should count for something, represent some last achievement for the side he'd backed since he first donned a military uniform. There was no point roosting in the jungle after hope was lost beyond recall.

He knew there was a world of difference between a sacrifice and simple suicide.

The river pilot barely spoke a dozen words to Bolan on their journey, moving steadily against the current. Bolan saw fat caimans basking on the muddy banks and made a mental note to watch for them if there were any rivers to be crossed on foot. He didn't fear the reptiles but respected them immensely and had no desire to nourish one of them with his own flesh.

The launch's engine suddenly sputtered, cycling down. The pilot steered in toward the eastern shore, choosing a point where branches overhung the water.

"This your place," the pilot said. "Good trails from here go all around. See many animals."

I'll bet, Bolan thought, as he answered, "Good."

"When you come back?" the pilot asked, showing a measure of concern for Bolan for the first time since they'd met.

"I can't be sure," Bolan replied.

"You have *telefono?*"

The warrior smiled at that. "I do."

The pilot reached inside his baggy shirt's breast pocket and produced a shiny business card. It bore his name, mailing address and a telephone number.

"You come back here again and want a lift, you call, okay? Same price."

"Sounds fair."

"If I not see you anymore, *vaya con díos,* eh?"

"*Vaya con díos,*" Bolan echoed. *Go with God.*

The pilot waited until Bolan was safely on the riverbank, then turned his launch and gunned the outboard motor, heading back downstream. He didn't raise a hand in parting or glance back at Bolan. They were done, unless he got a call one day to make a pickup on the river, at the same coordinates.

Vaya con díos, Bolan thought again, as he unwrapped his

rifle and his sidearm, double-checking each. A moment later, he was on his way.

The forest swallowed him alive.

"COMING."

The single word, almost whispered, still sounded like a shout to Paco Alvarez. Crouched in the jungle shadows with a rifle clutched against his chest, he almost raised a hand to cup the tiny earpiece of his two-way radio, for fear that his advancing enemies might hear the warning and retreat.

That was ridiculous, of course. They wouldn't hear it even if they stood beside him, bending to listen. Still, it made him nervous in the way he always felt before an ambush, knowing anything could happen and the trap could be reversed, crushing his soldiers and himself instead of those they meant to kill.

Regardless of his best-laid plans, the scheme could still backfire. These moments might turn out to be his last, in which case—

No!

Alvarez rejected that defeatist thinking, focusing instead on victory. The soldiers marching toward him, heedless of the danger to themselves, were little more than bullies hired to terrorize the rural peasantry. They had been trained to some extent but operated more on arrogance than any proper skill, expecting all to kneel or flee before them as if they were minor gods.

They had a lesson waiting for them.

Alvarez made no attempt to signal his guerrillas. They could hear the soldiers coming, would see them soon. Might even smell them if they'd been a few days in the bush, living on beans. Easing the safety off his M-16, he found a point of focus on the trail and held it, waiting for his prey to come to him.

The point man was a wiry fellow, ducking under vines and hanging branches, using his machete only when the vegeta-

tion would not let him pass by any other means. Still he was
not particularly quiet, seeming to believe that no inhabitant
of the surrounding greenery would dare to challenge him.

One last mistake.

Behind the scout came others, straggled out along the trail
in single file. It was impossible for Alvarez to count them from
his place behind a fallen tree, but he supposed there would be
twenty, more or less. Smaller patrols were rare, while larger
parties traveled mainly on the cleared roads with support from
armored vehicles.

Twenty or thirty men, all armed, presumably all killers.

Alvarez had sixteen men and the advantage of surprise.

He watched and waited, let the scout move past him down
the trail. Others would deal with the man when he gave the
signal and the killing started. One way or another, Alvarez was
confident that he would never see the scout alive again.

When three more men had passed him, clearly oblivious
to the danger, Alvarez picked out his target—a lieutenant with
a thick mustache—and sighted on his chest. The officer was
sweating through his olive-drab fatigues, muttering curses at
the heat and biting flies, the broad flap on his holster fastened.

Fool, Alvarez thought.

Alvarez had his rifle set for 3-round bursts. He stroked the
trigger and slammed the 5.56 mm tumblers through his target's rib cage at a range of less than thirty feet. Explosive impact hurled the lieutenant backward, nearly toppling the man
behind him as he fell.

At once, guns blazed along both sides of the game trail. Alvarez had placed his men at staggered intervals to keep them
from shooting one another. A blind man could have dropped
their targets at that range, he thought.

Some two-thirds of the startled soldiers fell without returning fire, cut down before they understood exactly what was
happening. The others made it interesting, but only just.

Firing in all directions, panicking, the soldiers tried to double back the way they'd come, but Alvarez had closed the door behind them. They could not retreat, could not proceed. Their only choice was to surrender or die fighting, and it hardly mattered since the GPLF took no prisoners.

Another moment of chaotic thunder finished it. The echoes died away, smothered by the encroaching forest, while the ambush party's members rose and closed in on their fallen enemies. Alvarez moved along the line of corpses, counting.

Twenty-two.

It was a good day's work, particularly in respect to captured weapons and equipment. They could always use more rifles, ammunition, knives, boots—anything, in fact, that could be liberated from the dead.

Only the bodies themselves had no value to him. They would feed the jungle's scavengers and finally the soil itself.

Alvarez bent to pluck an automatic pistol from the dead lieutenant's belt, then froze. A brisk vibration from the sat phone in his pocket made him pause. Only one caller had his number, and it wouldn't do to keep that caller waiting.

Smiling with the pleasure of his victory, Alvarez palmed the phone and spoke into its mouthpiece. "Alejandro," he began, "congratulations are in order."

"Never mind," Cruz said. "You have new orders."

Cruz could picture his second in command frowning at the news. If Alvarez had said there was a new disaster to report, Cruz would have listened, grudgingly, to weigh its impact on his own grim information. As it was, with yet another victory behind him, he anticipated no complaints about his latest plan.

"Of course, Chief," the small voice answered from his sat phone earpiece.

Cruz did not sugarcoat his news. "Santos Medina has been killed," he said. "The site may now be compromised. We need to harvest from it all we can, as soon as possible."

"I understand," Alvarez said.

Cruz did not ask where Alvarez was located, for fear of tipping off eavesdroppers. Rather, he inquired, "Do you know how to reach the site from where you are?"

"I do."

"Good. Proceed there at once," Cruz ordered. "Make the site secure. I'm bringing the main force to meet you there and liberate whatever still remains."

Cruz knew that Alvarez had to have a thousand questions, but like any good lieutenant speaking on an open line, he kept them to himself. Instead, he answered, "We begin at once."

"It may be late on Thursday when we reach you," Cruz continued. "Do not try to sort the goods yourself. I'll bring Tomas to judge their value."

"It shall be as you say," Alvarez replied.

Cruz severed the connection, turned back from the tree line where he'd gone to find some privacy, and watched his soldiers breaking camp. It had been time to leave in any case, although he hadn't planned on quite so long a march before they pitched their tents again. They faced a full day's hiking over game trails, through the worst of Guatemala's jungles, just to reach more jungle and begin an arduous, backbreaking task.

It could be worse, though, Cruz decided. It could just as easily have gone the other way—Medina still alive, and soldiers camped out on the treasure trove, waiting for Cruz and his guerrillas to return and walk into their trap. That would have been more subtle and effective, might indeed have finished him, but Cruz had a second chance.

Or did he?

It was possible, he realized, that enemies already held the site from which his unexpected riches came. They might be waiting even now with guns emplaced, to cut his men down as soon as they appeared. But Cruz and his main body would not be the first to reach the site.

Instead, as calculated, Alvarez would have that honor.

Cruz and Alvarez were the best of friends, had been for years, but strategy sometimes required a sacrifice. In this case, if the enemy *was* waiting, Alvarez could either crush them or, while dying, warn his comrades of the danger they faced. It was a noble mission, either way.

Cruz hoped his lieutenant would appreciate the opportunity.

And if he survived, there would be rich rewards for all. The treasure Cruz had sold so far was trivial, compared to what still lay in tombs and cellars excavated by a vanished race, long centuries before the present government drove its impoverished subjects to rebel. It was a gift of sorts, passed down from his forgotten ancestors to Cruz, just when he needed it the most.

Almost as if the Mayan ghosts endorsed his struggle, willing him to victory.

Cruz did not consider himself a superstitious man. Unlike so many Guatemalan peasants, he dismissed the tales of forest demons, evil spirits dwelling in the lakes, rivers and mountains. He believed the evil done by men was bad enough, and if a day of judgment ever came he knew he would have things to answer for. Still, in his own mind Cruz could never match the evil of his enemies. He was a saint beside the hypocrites and thieves who ruled his country with support from foreign states and corporations.

Was it possible that ancient Mayan spirits watched him from on high and *chose* him to receive their treasure for a worthy cause? Perhaps. But then again…

Cruz didn't need permission from the prehistoric dead to pick up riches that were left behind to rot in jungle tombs. He needed money to pursue his revolution, and a hoard of treasure had been found to meet his need. It would be madness to reject that gift and struggle on in poverty, thus dooming his campaign to failure. And whatever his opponents said about him, Alejandro Cruz was not insane.

His men were nearly ready. Cruz walked to the spot where they had broken down and packed his tent. A backpack waited for him and he shouldered it, picked up his rifle.

His war had reached a turning point. Cruz recognized that fact and welcomed it. Whatever happened in the next few hours—days at most—might well decide his fate and that of all his men.

Cruz shouted at his troops to get in line, make ready for the march. They hastened to obey, bringing a smile to his face.

"Move out!" he ordered sharply. "There is no more time to waste!"

9

Bolan's initial plan was to locate the spot where Howard Travis had been found, using a GPS device and the coordinates Brognola had supplied, then launch his search from there. He had no time limit in mind but reckoned that he'd know when the odds against him tipped over from the needle-in-a-haystack range to outright hopeless. He could also check with Stony Man Farm by sat phone, though in truth Bolan expected little help from that direction.

He'd considered taking on a native guide, but decided it would compromise his mission and an innocent civilian's life. If the location of Site X was common knowledge among local Indians and peasants, the trickle of artifacts sold outside Guatemala would've been a flood by now. The jungle would be crawling with treasure hunters and the soldiers sent to rein them in.

Bolan stayed alert for government patrols who would be curious, to say the least, about a gringo wandering around their country armed with military weapons, camou-painted face and jungle fatigues. Bolan had no good answers for the questions they were bound to ask him—if they didn't simply shoot him on sight.

The rifle he had chosen for his mission was a Steyr AUG, rated by most experts as the most accurate and durable assault rifle available. It weighed a half-pound less than the standard M-16, included a factory standard optical sight and grenade launcher, while its damage-resistant plastic magazines were transparent, allowing a shooter to count his remaining rounds at any time. The Steyr's effective range was ranked as shorter than the M-16's, and Bolan knew distance shooting meant nothing in jungle combat. The AUG carried forty-two rounds in its larger magazines versus the M-16's thirty. The AUG's bullpup design also made it five inches shorter than the M-16, thus easier to handle at close quarters.

The Beretta autoloader rode Bolan's web belt, together with a standard-issue Ka-Bar fighting knife, canteens, and spare magazines for the pistol. His other gear included British-issue fragmentation grenades, a sound-suppressor for the Beretta, two bandoliers of ammo for the AUG, a two-foot machete, a flashlight with a red lens cap to mask its beam at night and a substantial first-aid kit. In short, he was prepared for anything but failure.

Still, that might not be his call.

Preparation and determination were critical to any mission, but they didn't make a fighting man invincible or give him powers of discovery beyond the normal human range.

No matter how well armed or trained he was, Bolan might fail to find Site X.

And if he failed…then, what?

The GPLF would continue cashing in on ancient artifacts until the stash ran out or someone else discovered its location and took steps to close the pipeline. Either way, he doubted that the Mayan gold would help the rebels overthrow the government they hated, but it could fund new weapons and explosives, spread more misery around a country that had seen more than its share.

He spared only a passing thought for the American professor who had died seeking Site X. The man was on a quest that would've made him famous, in a region known to be extremely dangerous. It was unfortunate that he'd been murdered, and the Executioner would happily chastise his slayers if he got the opportunity, but Howard Travis had to have known the risks involved before he left his desk at Princeton to pursue the dream. The fact that it had turned into a lethal nightmare had no lasting relevance to Bolan's quest.

Based on his GPS readings, Bolan calculated that he was covering an average one mile per hour in the verdant jungle. Rain fell periodically and soaked him to the skin, then stopped as suddenly as it began, leaving Bolan to steam along with the rank vegetation around him. The soakings didn't bother him, since it was hot enough to ward off any threat of hypothermia, but they changed soil to muck beneath his boots and made for tougher going.

Slow and steady wins the race, he thought, and almost smiled.

He knew that wasn't true in most cases, of course. Speed might be deemed irrelevant in Aesop's fables but it often made the difference in real life, whether in combat or athletics. Even if he was the only person in the country looking for Site X, slogging through mud would soon sap Bolan's energy, exhaust him in a fraction of the time that marching over dry and open ground might do. Heat and fatigue would make him sweat more, drink more water, need to stop more often and replenish his canteens—assuming that he found clean drinking water as he roamed about the forest. Otherwise, he'd have to stop and boil whatever water he could find, regardless of its quality, which meant further delays and greater risk.

Bolan had traveled nearly six miles from the river on a steady northeast heading when a man appeared in front of him as if from nowhere, standing in the middle of the trail. They eyeballed each other for a heartbeat, Bolan taking in the stranger's features, the bandanna wrapped around his shaggy head and the automatic rifle in his hands.

Even if Bolan shot him first, the stranger likely could get off at least one blast and pepper Bolan where he stood. Buckshot at thirty feet could gut him, leave him dying on the muddy trail.

Another heartbeat passed before the stranger made his

choice and bolted, calling out to someone still unseen. Bolan grasped his one chance and took off running in the opposite direction, giving up the game trail for a slice of wilderness.

He hadn't found Site X, but someone had found him.

The hunt was on.

"A MAN? WHAT MAN?" Paco Alvarez demanded.

"Back there," the point man answered, index finger aiming at a spot where jungle swallowed up the trail. "A gringo."

"And you didn't kill him?"

"No, sir."

Alvarez slapped the scout, staggered the smaller man and almost knocked him down. "Why not?"

"I—"

"Never mind! Go after him! We'll follow you."

"He had a rifle, sir."

"All the more reason to kill him while you had the chance. Go, now!"

There was no longer any prospect of surprise, so Alvarez barked orders at his troops, made all the noise expected of an officer with a substantial force at his command. The gunman on the trail had only seen his scout. If he had company, let them believe that they faced overwhelming odds.

It never hurt to cheat a little when the stakes were life and death.

The scout was off and running, without a backward glance at Alvarez. His fear was useful. When he saw the stranger next time, he would fire immediately and be done with it.

Unless the unknown gunman killed him first.

Alvarez sent three other men along the trail behind the scout, then followed with the remainder of his troops. He knew enough of ambushes to balk at leading where a team of scouts could go instead. While not afraid to fight at any time, he saw no need to sacrifice himself as an example to his men.

What would they do without him, anyway? Most likely

double back toward Cruz's base camp, only to discover that it was no longer where they'd left it. Cruz was on his way to meet them at the treasure site, but none of Alvarez's men knew how to find it on their own.

A moment later, Alvarez saw one of the three men he'd sent to chase the scout, waiting to greet him in the middle of the trail. "What's happened now?" he challenged.

"Sir, I was told to wait and lead you."

"Lead us *where?*"

The soldier pointed from the trail into the murky forest. "There," he answered. "Carlos says the man he saw went that way. Javier and Rolo followed him."

"Only the one man, still?" Alvarez asked.

"So Carlos said, sir. I saw no one."

"All right, then. After them!"

His point man plunged into the jungle, sure-footed and swift. Alvarez followed, the rest of his guerrillas coming after him in single file. Given the choice, he would have opted for a skirmish line stretching from north to south, but that meant slowing, each rifleman maintaining contact with the men on either side of him.

There'd been no gunfire yet, which meant their quarry was escaping—or perhaps retreating toward a predetermined ambush site. He could be bait, a prospect that had crossed Alvarez's mind. Still, failing to eliminate him put the squad at risk and jeopardized its mission. If they let a stranger live, perhaps fall in behind and follow them, the secret of the GPLF treasure hoard might be exposed.

And friendship notwithstanding, Cruz would take a long time killing him if that occurred through any lapse on Alvarez's part.

Alvarez slogged through mud and clinging undergrowth, a string of silent curses ringing in his head. The jungle was his enemy, as much as any stranger on the trail or troop of soldiers sent from Guatemala City to destroy him. It was neutral, cared nothing for any of the petty struggles waged by human beings, but neutrality was hostile in a landscape where the smallest insect carried lethal venom or disease, where falling trees might crush a man or quicksand suffocate his dying screams.

Alvarez didn't know who he was chasing, but his scout could tell the difference between a gringo and an Indian or native peasant. If a gunman from the outside world had found his way into this forest, Alvarez was bound to kill him. No threat to the GPLF could be tolerated when their mission was already so precarious.

Alvarez caught himself clutching his rifle so tightly that his fingers tingled, on the verge of going numb. He willed his muscles to relax while keeping all his senses on alert. These were the moments when a heartbeat's warning made the difference between survival and an ugly death. The soldiers he had ambushed earlier that day could explain the difference, if they were still alive to talk.

Where *was* the man?

Granted, his scout had failed to take advantage of a perfect opportunity, but no man Alvarez had ever seen or heard of had the power to simply vanish in the time this gringo gunman had been granted. He could not turn into mist and let the faint breeze carry him away. A man of flesh and blood could only go so far, so fast, and there were always traces of his passing to be found by those whose eyes were trained.

Hurry! he urged the others silently. Find him, before it is too late!

BOLAN HAD GAMBLED on his instinct, held his fire for just a fraction of a second when confronted by the gunman on the trail, and he had been rewarded when the young man fled. Not far—that much was clear from all the noise he made, but still it bought the Executioner some time.

He didn't know the Guatemalan forest well, or this stretch

of it in particular, but jungles the world over shared some traits in common. If a soldier learned to hunt and hide in Asia, he could likely do the same successfully in Africa or South America. The worst mistake that he could make, however, was to underestimate the local talent.

That was one mistake Bolan *never* made.

While the jungle scout noisily gathered his friends, Bolan fled without panicking, used precious seconds to cover his tracks where he could, leaving other marks where they might dupe and mislead his pursuers. It wasn't a bet he could take to the bank, but rather the best he could do on short notice, in haste, without standing to fight.

If it came down to killing he knew how to do it, but Bolan preferred not to skirmish just now, when he still had so far left to go and so much yet to learn. Evasion was a perfectly acceptable alternative in this case, when he didn't even have a fix on who the hunters were.

The scout he'd seen wasn't a soldier in the ordinary sense. His uniform of odds and ends would never pass inspection in a standard military unit, and he didn't have the feel of rigid discipline about him. Certainly, he hadn't been prepared to kill on sight when suddenly confronted with a target that defied his expectations for the given place and time.

The scout's reaction might be Bolan's saving grace.

Or maybe not.

Behind him, he could hear the hunters coming. They'd abandoned anything resembling stealth, trusting in speed to compensate for their initial failure. Bolan took for granted that their knowledge of the killing ground had to be superior to his. If they pursued him long and hard enough, they'd catch him. He could only foil that plan by trickery—or in the last extremity, by turning on them with such fury that it broke their charge and cut them down.

The problem with that do-or-die scenario was that he didn't know how many hunters were pursuing him or how well they were armed and trained. He didn't want to pull a kamikaze stunt if he was critically outnumbered and outgunned. Raw nerve would only carry him so far, and if he overplayed that hand his life would turn into a busted flush.

As Bolan covered ground, he started looking for a place to hide. It wouldn't be an easily defensible location, since concealment and security were sometimes mutually exclusive. There was no time for him to construct a hide or stand. The landscape would have to provide his opportunity, or he'd be flushed from cover, forced to fight.

He heard water rippling over stones and other obstacles not far ahead of him. Bolan made for the sound and reached it moments later, standing on a grassy bluff above a stream as dark as coffee, twenty feet or so in width.

He jumped and landed in a crouch, turned back to smooth the grass and moss where he had stood. It wasn't perfect by a long shot, but it was the best that he could manage in the time available.

He searched the overhanging bank in front of him, eyes scanning twenty yards to either side. He nearly missed the cave, mistook it for a simple shadow at first glance, but moving closer found a muddy pocket in the soil that would accommodate his body with some room to spare. Approaching voices made the choice for Bolan and he wriggled into it, pulling the weeds upright where he had smashed them down and hoping no one looked too closely at the end result.

Vibrations in the damp earth told him when the hunters stood directly overhead. He heard their muffled voices, understanding every fifth or sixth word in the rapid-fire exchange, and gave up trying to make sense of it. He'd know it if they found his hiding place, and while he was prepared to fight, the hole in which he'd hidden offered no security from bullets or grenades.

Bolan went rigid, barely breathing, as a scout jumped from the bank above and landed several feet from his niche. Unless the man he'd seen before had stopped to change his pants, this was a second gunman, once again displaying no trace of a military uniform. Watching the hunter's legs stalk back and forth, Bolan clung tightly to his AUG, his index finger curled around the trigger. He could take one of them with him, anyway, before they started pouring fire into the cave and finished him.

The scout roved up and down the stream bank, facing the water, as if he expected to see Bolan swimming for his life or climbing up the other bank. Long moments later, with a negative report, he scrambled up the slope with aid from helping hands above.

Bolan lay waiting, thinking it had to be a trick, until the tremor of retreating footsteps faded. Even then, he spent another moment in his muddy hole, hoping to wait out any watchers that his adversaries may have left behind. At last it was too much for him, and he emerged to find himself alone.

The near-miss made him think. Bolan assumed the men who had pursued him were guerrillas. Why else were they armed with military weapons, chasing strangers through the forest? Working from that conclusion, it was likely they were affiliated with the Guatemalan People's Liberation Front. And if they *were* GPLF...

Without another moment's hesitation, Bolan scrambled up the sodden bank and followed those who had been stalking him short moments earlier. He didn't know where they were going, and it hardly mattered at the moment. All he needed was a chance to separate a likely prospect from the rest and question him, if that was possible.

And get a lead to send him on his way.

10

"I think is too much fire," Luis Candera said.

"Too much?" His young employer frowned. "We need to boil more drinking water, and the stew—"

"Too much," Candera said again, removing several of the sticks the woman had piled atop the fire before their bark burst into flame. "Smaller is better here."

"Explain," she ordered. While her tone did not convey the arrogance of other gringos Candera had been hired to serve, it left no room for argument.

"Small fire is good for water, food and keeping animals away. Big fire draws others we don't want."

"Others?"

Candera shrugged, trying to keep it casual. "Bad men come this way, sometimes. Not to worry. Just take care."

"Bad men," the woman echoed. There was something close to sadness in her face, where he'd expected fear.

"Maybe we don't see them," Candera said.

His client reached behind her pack and found the shotgun she had carried since they'd left Flores. "I almost hope we do," she answered.

There was a strength to this one that Candera had not noticed when she'd paid him for his services. He'd been expecting her to fold, call off the expedition and repent of ever setting foot in Guatemala's rain forest, agree to terms if he would only take her back to the fair land of showers and clean sheets.

But she had proved Candera wrong.

This one had steel beneath the soft exterior, and grim determination to locate whatever she was looking for. The woman hadn't shared that secret with Candera, even though he was her guide and theoretically responsible for her survival in the wild. Instead, after consulting a device she carried in her knapsack, *she* told *him* which way to go, charting their course and leaving Candera to handle the details.

It was strange, verging on eerie, how this young woman who didn't know the first thing about woodcraft could direct Candera through the jungle. She'd explained it when they met, but the details eluded him. Something about a satellite spinning among the stars. Candera didn't understand most of it, wasn't even sure that he believed it, but he *had* believed the woman's explanation that she needed someone with a master's knowledge of the jungle to convey her safely through it. Someone who could feed her, keep the animals from poisoning or eating her, keep her from stumbling off a cliff or drowning in a swamp before she reached her goal.

Luis Candera was that man.

His skills were unsurpassed, as he told anyone who'd listen. As for courage, he'd once grappled with a jaguar and survived to tell the tale—omitting the fact that the cat had run away after a few ferocious seconds, when Candera uttered an ear-piercing shriek and soiled himself. He was a marksman who could keep the pot full for his clients, and he'd never lost a customer.

Not yet.

The woman made him nervous, though. He didn't like the mystery surrounding her, the fact that she would only share her purpose with him when they reached their unnamed goal. It had the feel of an adventure to it, when Candera much preferred a simple business deal.

"What's in the stew tonight?" she asked, distracting him.

Candera smiled. "It's a surprise," he said.

"Not monkey meat again!"

He shook his head. "No monkey."

It was lizard, but Candera wasn't sure if he should tell her that. She had the constitution of a native, from what he had seen of her, but there were limits most Americans and Europeans couldn't overcome. There came a point on almost every job when Candera's employers gave it up and told him they had seen enough, had gone off roughing it.

But not the woman.

Not so far.

Candera felt a sneaking admiration for her, though he kept it to himself. He also worried that she might have come in search of something she could never find—some kind of absolution for her past, or something that would guarantee a bright tomorrow.

Neither miracle was hidden in the Guatemalan jungle.

There was only lurking death.

Candera saw the sadness in the woman, as if she lamented something she had lost. That sense had almost been enough to make him lie and say that he was busy, send her to another guide, but she had eased his qualms with cash. Now, as another day slipped into dusky shadows, he replayed that choice and wondered if he'd made a critical mistake.

Luis Candera didn't know where they were going or how long they should expect to be in transit, but he'd know when they had passed the point of no return.

Unfortunately, he knew by that time it would already be too late.

TRAILING THE WAR PARTY was easy, since it made no effort to conceal its tracks. The lead Bolan had given them allowed him to proceed without excessive stealth, using his ears to track his subjects while his eyes remained alert for any booby traps they might've left behind.

The jungle fighters seemingly gave no thought to the possibility that he might follow them. Once having lost him, they apparently assumed that Bolan would keep running for his life until exhaustion brought him down. He was surprised that they had given up so easily, but from the pace that they had set beyond the point of his encounter with the scout, he guessed that they had other business on their minds.

The question on Bolan's mind was whether he should intervene if the guerrillas launched into some kind of combat operation. They were either terrorists or liberators, all depending on the viewer's personal perspective, and Brognola hadn't launched him on a general campaign against the GPLF leadership. His moral compass told him that a man should always intervene with any means at hand to interrupt atrocities in progress—but if the guerrillas met a group of soldiers, say, and fought a skirmish in the jungle, would it be his place to interfere?

Or should he simply snatch one of the party's stragglers, carry him away and try to make him understand some basic questions while he had the chance?

It was a judgment call, and one unlikely to be tested in the present circumstances. Hiking through the forest, alternately drenched by rain and steaming in the heat, he had no reason to believe that any battle was impending. It was better for his purposes if the guerrillas simply camped and posted sentries, one of whom could disappear during the night without creating a commotion as he went.

That was the way to go, Bolan decided, if they gave him any choice.

An hour after missing Bolan at the stream, the party of guerrillas took a break. Bolan closed in to watch them, learned enough from eavesdropping to figure out that they were on a schedule, marching toward some kind of rendezvous. He didn't catch the rest of it but recognized their leader from his recent video briefing as Palmero "Paco" Alvarez.

Not bad, Bolan thought. Pure luck had placed him in the path of Alejandro Cruz's chief lieutenant, leading a commando team to who knew where. It might turn out to be a waste of time, but now that he had spotted Alvarez, Bolan began to tinker with his makeshift plan.

Instead of picking off a sentry and attempting to glean information the man might not possess, he would go for Alvarez himself. The risks were greater, but he focused on the payoff. Alvarez was much more likely to have key information than some flunky from the ranks. And, as the GPLF's second in command, he might even know where to find Site X. If not, smart money said that he could lead Bolan to Alejandro Cruz and help him get his answers from the horse's mouth.

The party's scouts had not been granted any rest. While Bolan watched the riflemen, hoping that Alvarez would slip into the forest to relieve himself, the same point man who had encountered Bolan on the trail returned with news. He didn't shout it out, but others echoed his discovery in terms Bolan was able to translate.

The scout had found a camp somewhere ahead.

Immediately, Alvarez got his people on their feet, ready to move. Exhorting them to double-check their weapons, Alvarez did likewise with his M-16, then followed as the scout set off in the direction they'd been traveling before their break. Bolan allowed the column to proceed until the last rebel was out of sight, then set off in pursuit.

The scout's report had clearly come as a surprise to Alvarez. Whatever sort of meeting he intended in the jungle, it was obvious that Alvarez had not expected it to happen yet. He had his soldiers primed to fight, which boded ill for any travelers they were about to meet.

Again the question passed through Bolan's mind—to intervene or not? He chalked it up to wait and see, leaving it there until he had an opportunity to judge the circumstances and participants. His primary goal was a one-on-one with Paco Alvarez, and Bolan wouldn't scuttle that objective without a compelling reason.

Twenty minutes passed, and he'd begun to wonder if the scout had lost his way or was hallucinating, when a shout somewhere ahead of him told Bolan that his guides had found the camp. He veered off course, increased his speed to parallel the rebel column, gaining ground while they were focused on whatever lay ahead.

The camp was small, one pup tent and a hammock slung between two trees, flanking a fitful cooking fire. Without the flame and smell of wood smoke, it would be an easy miss. The campers had drawn danger to themselves while trying to prepare their evening meal.

Who were they?

Alvarez was speaking to them by the time Bolan arrived and found his vantage point. One of the campers seemed to be an Indian, apparently no stranger to the forest, but his lone companion was so out of place that Bolan blinked in frank surprise.

A woman in her early thirties stood beside the fire, in front of Alvarez, clutching a pump-action shotgun in her hands. Around her, automatic weapons bristled, aiming at her shapely form from point-blank range.

11

Bolan had never seen the woman before, didn't know her from Eve, but the sight of her riveted him. She would've turned heads in any setting, but her present company and backdrop made her all the more striking.

And the 12-gauge she was holding didn't hurt.

She had no chance, of course, against a dozen automatic weapons. Even if she blasted Alvarez out of his boots, the other riflemen would shred her where she stood. Bolan could not risk intervention, though he might be able to avenge her if the worst scenario was realized.

Meanwhile, he thought it best to watch and wait.

The woman kept her shotgun trained on Alvarez and spoke to him in English. "Who are you, and why do you invade our camp with guns?" she challenged.

At her side, the Indian began to translate, but he'd barely gotten started when the GPLF's second in command replied, "I should ask *you* why you are in my country."

"*Your* country?" The woman made a scornful face. "I have permission to explore this area for Mayan artifacts."

That news appeared to startle Alvarez as much as it did Bolan. "So, you are a scientist? Show me your permits, then."

"As soon as you show me police credentials," she replied. When Alvarez said nothing for a moment, she produced a sneer. "I didn't think so."

Smiling, Alvarez half turned to indicate his firing squad, all weapons trained upon the woman and her Indian companion. "You see our credentials pointed at your heart, gringa, and at your friend. How many of us can you kill?"

"Just you," she answered. Bolan was impressed, despite the tremor in her voice.

"So be it," the rebel leader said, raising his left hand. "If you prefer to die…"

It would've been the time to shoot him, time to rock and roll and go down fighting, but the woman blurted out, "No, wait! What do you want?"

Alvarez paused, his hand still raised. "I represent the Guatemalan People's Liberation Front," he said. "We do not recognize the government that issues papers for outsiders to despoil our heritage."

"Despoil! I'll have you know—"

"For all *we* know, you are a spy sent to observe us and report," Alvarez said.

"That's utterly ridic—"

"By rights, I ought to shoot you now, but since I have a soft spot in my heart for lovely women, I prefer to satisfy myself…concerning what you've said."

She got the hint and scowled at Alvarez. "I told you, I have—"

"Papers, *sí*. Which, coming from officials who would love to see us dead, mean less than nothing."

"Well, I didn't bring my sheepskin with me, mister."

Puzzled, Alvarez replied, "I do not understand."

"Forget about it. If my permits don't mean anything, how can I prove I'm not a spy?"

"That is a problem," Alvarez acknowledged. "It requires some thought. Surrendering your weapons would do nicely for a start."

"And if I don't?"

Alvarez shrugged. "Then you'd be wise to shoot me now, but you will die in any case."

Bolan stood ready with his AUG, prepared to join the fight if she accepted Alvarez's challenge, but the tall brunette relented after ninety seconds, thumbed the safety on her gun and handed it to Alvarez.

Still Bolan waited, poised to fire, in case the rebels had some extra treachery in mind. If Alvarez ordered his men to fire, he would be dead before the woman and her sidekick hit the ground. If he had any other nasty little games in mind, Bolan was standing by to help discourage him.

But even with the snide leer on his face, Alvarez made no effort to accost the woman. Instead, he snapped an order at his men that sent them poking through the Spartan campsite, rummaging around inside the woman's tent and dumping out the contents of the Indian's backpack. They found nothing suspicious, other than the Indian's machete, and Alvarez fired off a blistering string of Spanish curses when one of his soldiers emerged from the tent with a grin on his face and a bra in his hand.

The woman didn't blush at that—not quite—but Bolan recognized her natural anxiety at being stranded in the jungle with a dozen rifle-toting men who might decide at any moment that she was fair game for their peculiar fantasies. So far, it seemed that Alvarez was able to control his men, but mutinies had started over less and Alvarez himself was clearly not immune to lust.

Bad news, Bolan thought, but he knew that any premature intrusion on his part would only make it worse.

Fatal, in fact.

The rebel who had found the bra also displayed a camera to Alvarez. He took it, turned it over in his hands as if he thought it would have "Spy Gear" printed on it somewhere, then remarked, "So, you are a scientist?"

"That's right," the woman answered. "An archaeologist. I photograph my finds before, during and after excavation."

"I know that spies take photographs, as well."

"And so do bird-watchers. Is there a point to this?"

"You'll come with me," Alvarez said, "until I have a chance to verify your story and decide what should be done with you."

"Go with you where?"

"Not far." Alvarez smiled. "You may find it interesting—as a scientist."

"Listen, I'm not about to let you take me anywhere," the woman said. "I'm an American and I demand to speak with someone from the U.S. Embassy."

Alvarez laughed. "Of course," he answered. "It will be my first priority. Meanwhile, however, you will do as you are told or suffer for your Yankee arrogance."

The brunette was about to speak again, but she thought better of it. At her side, the Indian looked grateful that she'd managed to control herself.

Five minutes later they were on the trail again, leaving the woman's camp abandoned with her gear scattered and left to rot. Bolan gave them another lead, then followed as the shadows of the afternoon lengthened toward dusk.

THE WOMAN'S STORY had a ring of truth to it, but if she was what she claimed to be—an archaeologist—it did not make life any easier for Paco Alvarez. He had considered killing her when she'd declared her purpose, but the thought was barely formed when he decided that decision should belong to Alejandro Cruz himself. They would be reunited soon, and Cruz could grill the woman to his heart's content before he issued orders for her disposition.

She would have to die, of course. That much was clear.

If she turned out to be an archaeologist, it likely meant that she had come to find and take away their treasure—and if she wasn't, then she had to be a spy. In either case, a Yankee woman who'd been kidnapped by the GPLF—as her government would doubtless have it—could not be allowed to spread the tale.

If she was swallowed by the jungle, simply disappeared without a trace…well, that was something that occurred in Guatemala on a daily basis. It would grieve her family, assuming she had any, and the U.S. Embassy might ask some questions, but the crazy woman would have brought it on herself.

The main thing was to find out who had sent her, what she knew, and what—if anything—she'd managed to report before her capture. She hadn't found the precious site as yet, that much was clear from her location and the fact that she possessed no artifacts. But if she had coordinates and had transmitted them to someone else…

Trudging along the muddy jungle trail, Alvarez scowled at the timing of Santos Medina's death in Guatemala City, coupled with the American woman's sudden appearance where she did not belong. A revolutionary's life was filled with paranoia, chiefly because someone or other was always plotting against him, and Alvarez was no exception to that rule. He didn't trust coincidence, preferring to suspect sinister hands at work behind the scenes. But did those hands belong to someone in authority?

Something was clearly out of place with that scenario. If agents of the state wanted Medina dead, they would have seized him at his shop or home and carried him away to prison, where he could be tortured at leisure and shot at the government's convenience. Police wouldn't have crept into his shop and killed him, fought a skirmish with guerrillas in the street and then fled like thieves in the night.

Neither, Alvarez thought, would the state send an Indian guide and a woman alone—much less an American woman— to loot the GPLF's treasure trove. If government officials knew where the cache was located, soldiers would descend in force to claim it as their own under the rule of law. The president would not hesitate to call a press conference and trumpet his achievement to the world at large.

Something was definitely wrong.

But what?

Cruz could decide that after he had spoken to the woman. By the time he finished with her, Alvarez and company would have a good head start on clearing out the ancient city, carting off whatever might have value to the struggle.

As for history, Alvarez had as much appreciation for the past as any man, but he was more concerned about the future. They could change it, with the proper tools in hand, and chart a new course for his homeland in the years ahead. Freedom was more important to his people than the leavings of a bygone race, destined to sit on dusty shelves in some museum.

The Mayan empire was a part of ancient history. It had no relevance to the oppression suffered by his people on a daily basis or the means required to set them free. Ends justified the means, in Alvarez's way of thinking. Children yet unborn would study him and Alejandro Cruz as part of history, and they would thank him for his contribution to their liberty.

Or not.

It was a fact of life that most young people took their rights and privileges for granted, without thinking of the price that had been paid along the way to set them free. Alvarez did not begrudge the next generation its youthful ignorance and egotism. He had been the same way in his own youth, but he'd learned his lesson the hard way, with a government boot on his neck.

And he would not permit slogans about heritage or history to leave that boot in place, crushing the very life out of his people while they toiled like slaves for brutal, wealthy masters.

Change was coming, and if long-dead Mayans could contribute to the revolution, then perhaps they might be worth a little something after all.

THE REBEL HUNTING PARTY hadn't been particularly cautious prior to picking up their hostages, but with the woman and the Indian in tow they took greater care. All noise was banned, apparently, and on the rare occasions when a member of the group forgot—cursing a twisted ankle, slapping at an insect—the offender earned a glare from Paco Alvarez that could've withered flowers.

Bolan followed as he had before, but not as closely, giving them some extra space. He had no real concerns about the hostages as long as they were marching through the trees. If Alvarez had wanted either of them dead it would've been a simple thing to kill them back at camp and leave the bodies as a gift to jungle scavengers. The fact that both were still alive meant that he either had some use for them or else was waiting to consult his boss. In either case, it bought them all some extra time.

When Bolan checked his compass and his GPS device, he found that they were still heading northeastward, toward Belize. He didn't know where they were going, but at present it remained the only game in town and he decided to stick with it, for the sake of the two prisoners if nothing else.

A rescue would be problematic on multiple levels. The numbers were dicey, for one thing, though Bolan had defeated larger hostile units. He didn't want to wipe out Alvarez's party. That would end whatever chance he had of learning something from them that would move him closer to his goal.

If he took the hostages, he could forget about abducting one of Alvarez's men and grilling him for information. There would be no time or opportunity for that, and even if he managed one successful raid against the GPLF team without a general bloodbath, they would be alert if he returned.

The hostages were a problem he had not anticipated. If he rescued them, then he'd be saddled with them in the middle of the jungle at a time when his most treasured asset was mobility. The woman claimed to be an archaeologist, and while that didn't necessarily mean she was looking for Site X, his intuition told him that her presence was likely no coincidence. The best that he could hope for, if the rescue didn't turn into a bloody shambles, would be for the Indian to take her back wherever she had come from, where she'd sit out the remainder of the game.

From what Bolan had seen of her in action, he had reason to believe the woman would resist a sideline seat.

Wherever they were going, Alvarez apparently did not intend to march on through the dark of night. As shadows lengthened in the forest, gobbling up whatever daylight made it through the canopy above, the column slowed, then stopped completely. Bolan took a chance, moved closer, and saw Alvarez dispatching scouts once more.

It was a brooding group that stood or crouched around the woman and her guide, leaning on weapons, ever watchful. Alvarez ignored the hostages and watched the trail ahead, where his point men had disappeared. Bolan hung back and watched the whole assemblage, ready as before to intervene at the first concrete sign of danger to the prisoners but spared by the inaction of their captors.

After twenty minutes, Alvarez's scouts returned and told him something that appeared to please the GPLF's second in command. Another round of orders got the rebels on their feet and more or less in line, ready to move. Bolan stood watching them as they proceeded, giving them a hundred-yard head start, then followed with exaggerated care.

If they were looking for a place to camp, as it appeared, Bolan supposed they would be even more alert to matters of security. He trailed them slowly, cautiously, and overtook them as the party settled in a semiclearing with a briskly flowing stream nearby.

While Alvarez pitched camp and posted guards, Bolan examined the terrain. He had sufficient cover to observe them through the night, no problem, and to follow them when they left. As for a soft probe of the camp, much less a double rescue, it would take all of the nerve and skill Bolan possessed.

As half of Alvarez's men stood guard, the other half pitched tents and searched for dead wood for a fire. Most of the tents were two-man affairs, showing a fair degree of wear, but one was larger than the others, obviously meant for Alvarez. Whether he'd try to share it with the woman was a question Bolan waited to resolve—and it was answered when the hostages were prodded toward a pup tent beside the leader's.

Problems.

Bolan took stock of the situation, knew he could do nothing safely while daylight remained, and settled in to wait. His growling stomach settled for some jerky and water, then subsided into silence.

Crouching in the jungle, thirty yards from where a cook fire blazed, Bolan watched night fall on the scene and draw the ring of darkness closer to his adversaries. Alvarez's men made no attempt to hunt for food, relying on whatever rations they already carried in their packs. Bolan caught whiffs of it as they prepared the evening meal, but he could not identify the scent.

He sat and waited for the night to pass and lull them into sleep.

12

The soup was thin but hot and savory, served in plastic bowls that surprised Carrie Travis, reminding her of something that she might've seen on sale at Wal-Mart. She'd been expecting army mess kits, maybe hand-carved wooden bowls like something from a Tarzan movie in her youth, and she felt a little foolish.

But her dominant emotion was fear.

Luis Candera sat beside her on the ground, sipping his soup a little at a time to spare his tongue from scalding. They had not been given spoons, but half the gunmen ranged around them likewise had no utensils. From watching them, Travis guessed that each man in the group had to supply his own apparel and equipment. Everything about them reinforced her first impression of a ragtag private army living hand to mouth.

So far, the Guatemalan People's Liberation Front had not impressed her as a military force, but that was cause for greater worry in itself. She'd come to Guatemala knowing that its soldiers sometimes ran amok, raped villagers, shot nuns and tourists, even though constrained in theory by the law and military discipline. What could she expect from rebels who despised the government and all its laws?

Candera shifted on the ground beside her, nudging her with an elbow to the ribs. "He's coming," her guide said.

She saw the leader of the rebels circling toward them from the far side of the fire. He paused along the way for fleeting conversations with his men, but soon approached and sat to her left, leaving Candera on the other side.

"I trust our humble food was satisfactory," he said.

"The food's all right," she answered. "But I won't pretend to like the company."

"You're angry with me," he stated. "That's only natural. But you must understand that this is not your country. It does not belong to you. You do not make the rules."

Travis bristled at that. "I never said—"

"Some in your country," he pressed on, ignoring her protest, "believe that Washington controls the Western Hemisphere by right, a gift from God above. Your presidents Monroe and Teddy Roosevelt had much to say about this in their time."

"That was a long—"

"And nothing changes, does it?" he continued, staring deep into her eyes. "Whatever happens in another country, the United States feels free to intervene and save the people from themselves—from true democracy. If Washington dislikes the end result of an election, they send troops and claim they are *restoring order*. If a sovereign leader arms his nation, Washington demands that he disarm or face invasion in the name of peace. America bombs villages and hospitals to wipe out terrorism. Washington teaches police and soldiers in my country how to torture women and children, to prevent the spread of communism. As an educated woman, you must know these things."

"Am I allowed to speak now?" Travis challenged.

"Be my guest."

"Half the events that you're describing happened well over a century ago. My grandfather was still a child when Teddy Roosevelt went galloping up San Juan Hill. I don't support all of the things America has done within my lifetime, but I didn't set the policy or send the troops, okay? I've tried to tell you I'm an archaeologist, not Mata Hari or an alternate for the Trilateral Commission. I'm here to look for Mayan artifacts, not interrupt your war games."

"But you're searching for them in a war zone," he replied, "which is suspicious, as I'm sure you will agree."

"I'm following a trail of clues in search of history," she said. "It's not political."

"In Guatemala," he corrected her, "there is no separation between life and politics. Our government, supported generously by your own, decides who will survive and who will die. It allocates most of the land and power to an undeserving few, while the majority must labor as their slaves for wages that would not support a hamster in your country. Life is politics in Guatemala. Life is *war*."

"You have my sympathy, for what it's worth," Travis replied. "But all I want—"

"Is to discover ancient treasure, pose for smiling photographs, write articles," he said. "Perhaps have stories written about you."

"You don't know me," she told him angrily.

"That's where you're wrong," he said. "I've known Americans like you since I was old enough to walk. You smile and talk about the welfare of my people, but you mostly take, and what you give goes to the men whose boots are on our necks."

"And I keep telling you—"

"You're not political," he interrupted, almost sneering. "Fortunately, gringa, the decision on your fate will not be left to me. If you convince my chief that your purpose in this land is innocent, perhaps you will be spared."

She steeled herself and answered, "If he's anything like you, why don't you shoot me now?"

Beside her, Travis felt Candera cringing, as if waiting for the bullet, but their captor actually smiled. "You do have spirit," he observed. "I give you that. Unfortunately, that won't be enough. Spirited enemies are the most dangerous of all."

"I guess you'll want a good seat at the execution then," she countered, making no attempt to veil her personal contempt.

"You had it right the first time, gringa," he informed her.

"Executions in the Guatemalan People's Liberation Front are carried out by firing squad."

THE SMALL BAND of guerrillas didn't linger over supper. They were done and had their bowls washed up by half-past eight o'clock, guards posted and the prisoners secure inside their tent by nine. Aside from roving sentries—three in all, one-quarter of the team—the others turned in early, keeping rifles close beside them in their tents, hammocks or bedrolls.

Bolan didn't know how long the sentries were supposed to walk their beats without relief, but he assumed that Alvarez would time the shifts to give his men a fair amount of sleep. Three hours, say, which meant a changing of the guards at midnight and again at three a.m., to man the graveyard shift.

He settled in to wait and test his theory, knowing that the first-shift sentries would be more alert than their successors. They were wide awake, thinking about the hostages and what the morning would bring, fearful of an attack by enemies. The later watchmen would be groggy, newly roused from sleep and lulled into a false sense of security because the first shift hadn't been attacked.

That wouldn't make his job a milk run, but it would help his chances.

Bolan waited in the darkness as he had so many times before, watching his enemies, charting their movements, filing mannerisms in his mind for future reference. Given the choice, he didn't plan to kill these men this night, but if they met another day...

At straight up midnight, by his watch, two of the sentries moved to wake their replacements, while the third remained on guard. As Bolan had expected, the new guards were slower off the mark, carried their rifles slung or tucked beneath their arms, and generally didn't seem to think the gig was worth their time and effort.

He gave the three of them an hour to get bored, while those

they had replaced drifted into the netherworld of sleep. Then, creeping silently from where he'd lain to watch them, Bolan made his slow way from the tree line toward the tent that served the rebels as a makeshift jail.

By then, he had discovered that the three guards on the second shift stopped short of circling the entire perimeter. Each had a post from which he wandered slowly back and forth, scanning the jungle between yawns and periods of staring at the campfire or the stars. They never actually met or made a total circuit of the camp. The prison tent stood midway between what Bolan thought of as the first and second sentry posts, consigned to no-man's-land.

Perfect.

He hugged the shadows, took his time, running the numbers in his mind with no need to consult his watch. If all went well, he and the liberated prisoners would have the better part of ninety minutes on the trail before the next shift change, and some three hours after that before the camp at large was roused to find them gone.

If all went well.

And if it didn't, he would have to try Plan B.

Scorched earth.

It wasn't Bolan's first choice, though he reckoned he could pull it off. Job one was still location of Site X, a task that Alvarez and company might help facilitate if they were still alive. Freeing the prisoners was incidental, something done for Bolan's peace of mind with no real hope of a material reward.

Site X was still his primary concern.

He reached the tent and drew his knife, was careful when he pierced the canvas not to pop it. Slowly, almost silently, he slit the tent's rear panel to create another flap and wormed his way inside.

The Indian sat staring at him, fists clenched in his lap, a brooding silhouette against the outer firelight showing through the tent. Deprived of his surprise, Bolan could only hope for luck.

"American," he whispered. "Help for you."

The silent shadow thought about it for a heartbeat, then nodded. Without delay, the guide moved to all fours, then pressed one hand over the woman's mouth and simultaneously whispered in her ear, "Wake up, Missy. We go now, very quiet. Yes?"

The woman craned her neck to catch a glimpse of Bolan, round eyes going wider when she saw his knife, the rifle slung across his back. Bolan saw her making a concerted effort to relax. She didn't struggle, simply nodded with the guide's hand still pressed to her lips.

"I'm going first," he told the pair. "You'll have to crawl. Stay low and take your time, but not too much. Above all, keep it quiet. Understood?"

Both hostages nodded.

The Executioner backed out of the tent, more vulnerable now than he had been at any time since entering the camp. If either of the nearby sentries glimpsed him, they could aim and fire before Bolan could reach his pistol. And after that, it wouldn't matter much what happened to Site X, as far as Bolan was concerned.

But no one glimpsed him as he wriggled from the tent, or as he drew the black Beretta. With his free hand, Bolan signaled for the prisoners to follow him, then started crawling toward the tree line, watching left and right like a spectator at Wimbledon as he proceeded.

When he had reached the cover of the trees, he rose and found a vantage point where he could watch both guards at once, tracking the progress of the liberated hostages. At one point, when the sentry on his left strolled off to urinate beyond the firelight, Bolan nearly dropped him, fearing the man would turn and spot the woman crawling midway from her tent to freedom, but the lookout had more pressing matters on his mind.

The native guide came last, moving with greater speed

and confidence than his employer. When they stood together in the jungle, Bolan leaned in kissing-close and whispered to them, "Follow me. No noise. Watch where you step."

More nods, and he turned from them, leading their retreat until the camp and firelight dwindled out of sight. They weren't safe yet, by any means, but they were getting there. If they survived the night, Bolan would have to think of what to do with his new companions while he proceeded on his way.

To find Site X and sweep its treasures out of rebel hands.

13

When they had covered a safe distance from the rebel camp and stopped to rest, the woman challenged Bolan for the first time.

"Look," she said, sounding a little winded, "I'm as grateful as can be, but if it's not too much to ask—hell, even if it *is*—I'd like to know who you are and exactly what the hell is going on!"

"The men who kidnapped you are members of a revolutionary group, the Guatemalan People's Liberation Front," Bolan replied.

"I know that much," she said. "They introduced themselves. Now what about—"

"I'm an American like you," Bolan pressed on. "Knowing the way the GPLF operates, I couldn't leave you in their hands."

"American, I'll grant you," the woman said. "But you're not like me. Not even close. You're some kind of soldier by the look of you, and how you staged our getaway. Are we at war with Guatemala, now?"

"I'm here on business," Bolan answered.

"Let me guess. The cloak-and-dagger kind?"

"Your main concern right now is getting out of here," he said. Casting a glance toward her companion, who had yet to speak since crawling from the GPLF camp, Bolan inquired, "Is this your guide?"

"He has a name," the woman said. "Luis Candera."

"And I'll ask again—"

"Yes, he's my guide. What of it?"

Bolan turned and asked Candera, "Can you get her back to Flores without any further trouble?"

"I think yes," the Indian replied.

"Now wait a minute! I'm not going anywhere," the woman said, "until I get some answers. Starting with your name."

"Matt Cooper," Bolan said.

"Okay, I'm Carrie Travis. I'm—"

"An archaeologist," Bolan said, hoping that the jungle shadows masked his frown. *Travis.* He doubted whether it could be coincidence.

"My God!" she said. "You have a *file* on me?"

"I overheard you talking to the man in charge," Bolan corrected her.

"Oh, well…You heard me? You were watching when they came into our camp?"

"Let's just say I was in the neighborhood," Bolan replied.

"My God! How long…you didn't… Did you see me at the stream this afternoon?"

"I missed that pleasure," Bolan said. "I've spent most of the day trailing the men who kidnapped you."

"What for?"

"That falls under the heading of my business," he responded, turning to Candera once again. "You should get started now, if you can find your way by night. They probably won't miss you until daybreak."

"We go now," the guide assured him.

"No, we don't," the woman contradicted, stepping closer as she challenged Bolan. "Listen, as I said, we're grateful for your help. But I have work to do—important work—and I'm not giving up because of this."

"You've lost all your equipment and supplies," Bolan reminded her. "In fact, all you've got left is what you're wearing. It'll be a big enough adventure for you getting back to Flores in one piece."

"Adventure? You think I'm some kind of dilettante?" she asked him, fuming. "Well, you'd better think again. I'm well respected in my field and I have work to do. I'm on a schedule, with permission from the Guatemalan government—"

"They didn't help you much this afternoon," Bolan observed.

"A glitch," she said. "We're safe now, and Luis can find the way back to our camp."

"Which is the first place the guerrillas will go looking for you when they miss you in the morning," Bolan said.

"You think so?"

"It's what I'd do," Bolan answered.

"But they're in a hurry," she replied. "Going to meet the man in charge, I'd say, from what I gathered."

"Taking you to see him," Bolan added. "So you'll be missed."

"But if they double back, they'd lose the best part of another day," Travis retorted.

He changed the subject. "Did they give you any indication where they might be going? Place names or coordinates?"

"Nothing like that."

"Okay." He faced Candera once again. "You'll likely have to hike all night and well into tomorrow. Do what you can. If they come after you, I'll slow them down."

"I've told you, I'm not going anywhere," Carrie Travis said, standing firm.

"You have a job to do," he answered. "I get that. But I'm curious to know why you're hell-bent on getting killed."

"That's not the plan, all right?"

"Your plan was shot to hell the minute Paco Alvarez and his men walked into your camp. It's time for you to put your job on hold and think about survival."

"You know the man who kidnapped us?"

"By reputation," Bolan said. "He's not someone you want to trifle with."

"Thanks for the tip. I'm still not leaving."

"Then he'll kill you," Bolan told her. "Or the jungle will. There's no Tarzan to swing down from the trees and save you when you're starving, bitten by a snake, or burning up with fever. If you stay, under the present circumstances, don't expect to see your university again. Someone may find your camp a week or year from now and send your field notes back, assuming they're intact, but that won't help your family."

"I've got no family," she flared. "Not that it's any of your business, Mr. Cooper."

"So that's it," Bolan said.

"That's *what?* If you've got something on your mind, why don't you spit it out?"

"It makes no sense, you know," he said.

"*You* make no sense. What are you—"

"Carrie, getting killed won't bring your father back."

"CHIEF, COME QUICK!"

The call roused Paco Alvarez from a disturbing dream in which he was pursued by hulking, snarling shadows in the forest. Time and time again he tried to kill his adversaries, but his rifle sputtered uselessly, as if the ammunition was defective, bullets spitting out like melon seeds and dropping to the ground.

He jerked upright, gasping, just as the sentry thrust his head inside the darkened tent, firelight behind him casting the young man in silhouette. "Chief?"

"The whole world hears you," Alvarez replied. "What's wrong?"

"The prisoners, they're gone!"

Alvarez bolted from his bedroll, remembering just in time to duck his head and keep from scraping it along the ridge-line of the tent. Snatching his rifle from its place beside him, he followed the sentry through a camp already roused by the alarm, until they stood before the pup tent where their hostages should have lain sleeping until dawn.

Alvarez poked his head inside, confirmed that it was unoccupied, then quickly found the slit they had cut in the back panel of the tent. He was raging by the time he crawled backward, out of the tent, and faced the soldiers gathered there.

"We searched them both," he stormed at no one in particular. "Where did they get a knife?" Those words were barely spoken when another thought occurred to him. "Who watched this part of the perimeter? Answer at once!"

The sentry who had come to fetch him raised a trembling hand. "It is my sector, sir. I discovered they were gone."

"And how long have you been on watch?" Alvarez asked.

"Since midnight, sir."

A quick glance at his wrist showed Alvarez the time. "It's five minutes past two," he noted. "Did you check the tent immediately, when you went on duty?"

"No sir," the guard replied. "My job was to—"

"Secure the camp!" Alvarez snapped. "So, tell me, did the prisoners slip past you, or were they already gone when you reported for your watch?"

"Sir, I don't…they…I believe they were already gone."

"You're lying!" another soldier said from the sidelines. Then, to Alvarez, "I had the watch before him, sir. Both were still inside the tent when he relieved me."

"Are you certain?" Alvarez replied. "How often did you check them?"

"Well…"

"How often did you look inside the tent?"

"Inside the tent? Sir, I— "

"Idiots! The pair of you are idiots! How can we hope to win a war with such as these?"

His first impulse was to unleash a rain of automatic fire and kill both useless sentries where they stood. But, since they represented nearly one-fifth of his total manpower, he'd have to let them live. For now.

"Since you are both incompetent," he raged, "we have no

way of knowing when they fled or how far they have traveled. Tracking them is hopeless in the dark. As for tomorrow…"

They would have no time to waste, he realized, with Cruz, Aguirre and the others marching toward their jungle rendezvous. Nearly irrational with anger, Alvarez stood with his rifle, clutching it so tightly that his knuckles blanched.

"They're lost to us," he said at last. "Whatever vital knowledge they possessed is gone. And you two," he addressed the frightened guardsmen, "will explain that loss to the commander."

Cringing from him, glancing briefly at each other, the two sentries might have bolted if they'd had the chance.

"Seize them!" Alvarez barked. "Disarm them and place them under guard. The man who lets one of them slip away will pray for death a thousand times before it comes."

He watched the others grapple with the two condemned men, stripping them of weapons, holding them at gunpoint while a rope was found to bind their hands, link them together with a loop around each slender waist, and tie them to a nearby tree. He'd let them spend the few remaining hours of darkness standing, and when they set out, Alvarez would march them tethered like a pair of slaves.

The walking dead.

Of course, their sacrifice would only go so far toward helping him. He was in charge of the patrol, and as the GPLF's second in command he had more personal responsibility than any of his men. It could go badly for him, when he told Cruz of the woman and her getaway. If Cruz was in a mood to make examples, three men might be shot as readily as two.

So be it.

There was nothing Alvarez could do about the problem at the moment. He'd taken prisoners and lost them, their importance to the movement still unknown. He might downplay the woman's self-description as an archaeologist, but if he did that and it proved to be a vital clue—if his duplicity should somehow be revealed—there would be no escaping drastic punishment.

Better to tell the truth then, trusting his friendship with Alejandro Cruz to spare him from a firing squad or worse. With any luck, Cruz and Aguirre would be busy with the treasure, too preoccupied with moving it to waste time on a court-martial.

With any luck.

Alvarez could not escape a feeling that his luck had all run out. First came the grim news that Medina had been killed, followed by orders to assist in clearing out the treasure site. Finding the woman and her guide had indicated more bad fortune on the way, to his mind, and the threat was amplified by her mysterious escape.

What next?

The next day would tell him that, if he survived that long.

A sudden thought struck Alvarez. What if the woman and her Indian were not alone? They had been searched for knives and tools, yet still their tent was slit. What if—

"We're breaking camp!" he shouted at his men. "Pack up your gear. We leave in fifteen minutes. Stragglers will be shot!"

"What do you know about my father?" Carrie Travis demanded. Her tone and expression mixed shock with outrage.

Bolan wasn't sure how far to push it, but he took a shot. "I know he was an archaeologist, like you. I know that he was murdered recently, not far from where we're standing. And it wouldn't be a huge stretch if I thought you might be following his footsteps."

The woman's eyes were brimming with tears, but there was steel beneath the emotion. "So you were lying," she replied. "There *is* a file on me. You're here because of what happened to Dad."

"You're half right," Bolan said. "I'm not aware of anyone who doesn't have a file somewhere, but if you've got one, I have yet to see it. I was briefed about your father's death, but I'm not here to find his killers."

"Oh? Why, then?"

"That's need-to-know," he told her bluntly, "and you don't."

"Excuse me?" Anger had almost completely shoved her sadness to the sidelines.

"I'm not a cop," Bolan replied. "And if I was, I'd have no jurisdiction here. I can't arrest your father's killers, even if I find out who they are. That job belongs to someone else, assuming they're prepared to do it."

"He's just a gringo, right? He brought it on himself."

"Like you, by meddling in the middle of a war zone where the paperwork you're carrying doesn't mean much to either side."

"Meddling?" She took a step closer to him, then thought better of it and retreated half a pace. "Need I remind you I'm a scientist? I have diplomas on my wall to prove it."

"In the States," Bolan said.

"Yes. Where most people at least pretend they're civilized." The words were barely out before she turned to face her native guide, saying, "I'm sorry, Luis, honestly."

"De nada, señorita."

"You should go home while you can," Bolan suggested. "If you hang around, there may not be another chance."

"You're saying I should just give up my father's work? His dream? I should forget about his death and just pretend none of it ever happened?"

"I never met your father, but I doubt that any of his dreams included being slaughtered in the jungle, much less having you die here on his behalf," Bolan said.

"You bastard!"

"Am I wrong?"

"Of course he wouldn't want… Listen. There may be some way I can help you. We can work together. Think about it."

Bolan looked her up and down, appraisingly, before he asked, "What is it you'd be bringing to the table?"

"Not my body, if that's what you're thinking!"

"I can promise you," he said, "there's nothing further from my mind."

"All right, then. I have knowledge of the area," she said.

"You didn't know there were guerrillas," Bolan told her, "and you couldn't stay out of their way."

"I'm not a soldier, granted. I'm—"

"A scientist," he finished for her. "We've established that. "And if I had a research paper pending, maybe you could lend a hand. But as it is, you're just a liability to everyone around you."

He imagined angry color rising in her cheeks, although the jungle shadows painted her in shades of black and gray.

"I know more than you think," Travis replied. "You know about my father's death. I think it brought you here, somehow, whether you will admit the truth or not. And you were right about my following his tracks. I want his killers *and* solutions to the mystery he gave his life to solve."

"What would that be?" Bolan asked.

"I suspect you know that," Travis said. "Site X."

"You have coordinates?" he asked.

"Just pointers, but smart money says I'm still ahead of you. I'm not the one who's following a bunch of Communists around the country, hoping that they'll lead me somewhere."

Bolan didn't trust her. He was more or less convinced that Travis would say anything, risk anything, to find her father's murderers and realize his dream of locating Site X. That quest had nearly killed her already, but if she *did* have a solid lead on how and where to find the site, it might be worth the risk of taking her along. Assuming that she understood the risks and volunteered, of course.

Sending her back with just her native guide could be as risky in the long run, Bolan reasoned, as allowing her to tag along with him. And he could always put her out of action, one way or another, if she threatened any aspect of his mission. He could tie her to a tree, or take any other measures necessary to complete his task.

"All right," he said at last. "Convince me."

14

Alejandro Cruz woke early, with the first gray light of dawn still well concealed beyond the looming forest canopy. A couple of his men were starting to revive their campfires from the night before, prodding the embers, adding whatever tinder they could find.

Cruz had left orders for an early start, but not this early. Normally, he would've slept until the breakfast preparations were proceeding and mouthwatering aromas drifted through the camp, but he had not enjoyed a peaceful night. Bad dreams had haunted him, made worse because he could remember none of them on waking. Cruz was left with nothing but a dark sense of anxiety, and he required no high-priced dream analysis to understand that feeling.

He was worried, certainly, about Medina's death and the attendant slaughter of his men in Guatemala City. Overnight he'd tried to solve the riddle and recalled the gringo Alvarez had executed on his order, several weeks before. Some kind of scientist, the man had claimed to be, and said the same thing even when persuasion was applied.

It all came back to treasure from the Old Ones and the difference that it had made in Cruz's life. Before the jungle yielded up its ancient bounty, he'd been struggling to make ends meet, living hand to mouth off the land and the generosity of sympathetic peasants, counting in his mind the weeks—then days—before the Guatemalan People's Liberation Front would waste away. His men were not afraid to die in battle, but they didn't want to starve for no good reason, huddled in the wilderness.

All that had changed with the discovery of ancient ruins in the jungle, overgrown and lost to memory, concealed from prying eyes for centuries on end. Its late unveiling had been accidental, the importance of it minimized until the first tomb seal was broken and a wealth of golden glory was revealed. As Cruz now knew, some of the ugly hand-carved stones and tablets were more valuable to collectors than the gold and silver artifacts or sparkling gems, but he was not well educated in such matters. It had taken the gold to catch his interest and make Cruz see what the discovery could mean to him.

And to his movement.

Almost overnight they had new weapons and equipment, better food and medical supplies, even a lawyer in the capital who represented GPLF members when they were arrested. Such defense was futile, but it made the men feel better, knowing that he'd tried to help them at the end. He'd even set aside a small fund for the families of men who stood against the wall, though most of them had no families.

All that was threatened now, and the most galling part for Cruz was that he didn't know his enemy by name. The government wanted him dead, of course, but none of this so far had gone according to their style. He saw another hand at work but couldn't name its owner, and that rank uncertainty disturbed him.

Crawling from his tent, Cruz stretched and listened to his joints crack, one after the other. Jungle life and war games were taking their toll. He wasn't as old as Castro, when he came down from the hills to claim Havana. But he had begun to feel the miles that passed beneath his boots and count the nights spent hunched over a campfire, slapping at mosquitoes when they came to sip his blood. Sometimes Cruz thought about the treasure and could not resist imagining himself alone, reclining on a beach somewhere beyond the reach of enemies.

The best revenge is living well.

Who said that? he wondered. Likely some American who never lived badly in the first place. Still, there was a ring of truth about it, and it taunted him.

I could go now, he thought.

They'd banked enough to get Cruz out of Guatemala, set him up somewhere in modest luxury, but two things held him back. The first was loyalty to his soldiers and their cause, though sorely tested by a series of defeats that left him half convinced their mission was impossible.

The second stumbling block was his belief that nothing should be done halfway. If he was going to forsake his home-land and his conscience for a life of hedonistic gluttony, Cruz didn't want to do it on a budget. He could always leave enough behind with Alvarez to keep the movement going for a while, and take the rest.

The lion's share.

Why not? Cruz asked himself, as he surveyed the slowly waking camp. What did he owe the people of his country who would not support him, even though he knew most of them loathed the present government? If they were cowards fright-ened into silence or accomplices in the corruption that despoiled his country, why should Cruz care what became of them?

That begged another question. Did he care?

There'd been a time when he could swiftly and emphatically respond to that question with a resounding "Yes!" But now…

Something to think about, Cruz told himself. There's no decision called for at the moment. Wait and see.

Returning to his tent, Cruz fetched his web belt, buckled it around his waist, the pistol in its holster heavy on his hip. He could remember life without a gun always at hand, and in those vague rose-tinted memories it seemed enticing.

Both campfires were blazing, and Cruz smelled coffee brewing. In another hour they'd be on their way to the forgotten city and its waiting treasure hoard. By early afternoon, the gold could be within his grasp.

He could be free.

"Just wait," he whispered to the jungle darkness. "Wait and see."

BREAKFAST FOR BOLAN and his two companions was an MRE split into thirds, with water and some greens Luis Candera gathered near their camp. The Army rations would've been more palatable warm, but they had passed the night without a fire and Bolan didn't want the scent of wood smoke bringing trackers down upon them after sunrise.

He was half convinced that Paco Alvarez had given up on hunting them, but fifty-fifty odds were nothing to write home about. Better to play it safe, in Bolan's view, than to regret a lapse in judgment with his dying breath.

They were in motion by the time the first pale rays of sunlight found their way through holes in the jungle canopy. He didn't like it, but it seemed to be the three of them together for a while. At least until the killing started, and he had to work alone.

As reluctant as he was to travel with civilians, he had been swayed by the woman's arguments about Site X. She had her father's notes and conversations virtually memorized, suggesting a location. And her guide—a lifelong native of the area—came recommended as the best available. Between them, Travis was convinced that she could realize her father's dream of locating the Mayan city. Alvarez had interrupted her within a day or two of reaching the location she'd projected, but between Luis Candera and the GPS device, she still seemed convinced of her ability to find it.

Bolan had agreed, despite misgivings, since his only real alternative was trailing Paco Alvarez around the countryside, in hopes the rebels might eventually lead him to Site X—or, as it seemed more likely, to the lair of Alejandro Cruz. That brought him back to kidnapping, interrogation, and a possibility that he'd get nothing out of it despite the risks involved.

So he was hiking through the Guatemalan jungle with a native and a woman whose allure was not greatly diminished by the rigors of the trail. Bolan enjoyed watching her walk in front of him, Candera in the lead, but he did not allow the slow gyrations of her rump in khaki trousers to distract him from his mission or the dangers it entailed.

At some point he would have to make it clear—Travis would have to take a back seat, clear his line of fire and let him do his job without distractions. He supposed Candera might be useful in a fight, but Carrie Travis would be excess baggage even in the very best scenario. And she would likely fight him if his only option was to finally obliterate the place that had lured her father to his lonely death. Bolan knew he would have to deal with anything that happened, but he definitely wasn't looking forward to it.

When the crunch came, he would do what had to be done.

But first, they had to find Site X.

It struck him that the exercise might be a costly waste of time. If Travis had misjudged her own abilities, misunderstood her father's clues, they could be trapped in a pathetic snipe hunt going nowhere. All her confidence seemed heartfelt and sincere, but she could be sincerely *wrong*.

It was a gamble, sure, but Bolan had to take a chance on someone, somewhere, or he'd never reach his goal.

And if they found Site X, then what?

He'd have to play that one by ear. Brognola hadn't been interested in what happened to the Mayan treasure, just as long as it stayed out of rebel hands. Beyond that, it was Bolan's call.

Assuming that he found the treasure to begin with, then survived to cast his vote concerning disposition of the spoils, he hoped the government would not become involved. He had no wish to contest the find with soldiers from the capital. Travis could deal with the red tape and politics, if there was anything worth fighting over when the smoke cleared.

And in the meantime, he would try to keep the archaeologist from getting killed.

It was the least—and best—that he could do.

Luis Candera walked the point without apparent effort. He had huddled over breakfast with his boss, received instructions, nodding and commenting as she went along, correcting her on certain points related to geography. Apparently, the standard map she'd memorized was missing certain features known only to natives on the ground—a river and a swamp for starters, one of which they'd have to cross, the other hopefully avoid.

So much for best-laid plans.

But they were on their way, which had to count for something any way he sliced it. The archaeologist's confidence was almost strong enough to be infectious, although Bolan generally found himself immune. Candera, for his part, had not seemed anxious to desert his paying customer.

Bolan had no idea if victory or death was waiting for them in the jungle ahead, beyond his line of sight.

He'd have to wait and see.

15

By the time his men had finished breaking camp, Paco Alvarez had memorized a rough outline of the story he would tell Alejandro Cruz. Lies on the major points would only trip him up and lead him to disastrous consequences. He would tell the story straight—up to a point.

His squad had found a Yankee woman in the forest with a native guide. She claimed to be a scientist but had not said what she was searching for. Alvarez had placed them under guard but they had managed to escape, thanks to a sentry who was half-asleep on duty. Alvarez had chosen not to hunt them since his team was small, the jungle vast and he was under binding orders to meet Cruz as soon as possible. The whole thing was unfortunate, a clear-cut case for discipline, but the escapees were unlikely to survive the jungle in their present state—unarmed, without supplies—and they had no significance to any of the GPLF's plans in any case.

It might not be an easy sell, but Alvarez believed that he could make it work. Cruz was agitated and distracted by events in Guatemala City, too distracted even to appreciate Alvarez's annihilation of another government patrol. The latest incident might feed his paranoia, but with skillful handling his attention could be redirected to the most important job at hand.

It should be relatively simple, overall. No one would speak in favor of the guards who had allowed the captives to escape.

Alvarez would frame the case his way, omitting any implication that the woman had come looking for their treasure hoard, but if Cruz reached the same decision independently, Alvarez would minimize the risk. Assuming that the woman managed to survive her jungle trek, against all odds, it would take days for her to reach the nearest telephone. By that time Cruz and Alvarez would have removed the treasure from its hiding place and stashed it somewhere safe.

Distracted by his private thoughts, Alvarez stepped down on a twisted root and nearly lost his footing, lurching like a drunken man for several steps. The men around him took care not to laugh, but Alvarez surprised them with his own quick grin and small, self-deprecating head shake, just enough to break the tension.

Alvarez pressed on, taking more care where his feet were planted, while his mind ranged on ahead of him, into the coming hours. He was on alert for problems more compelling than a tree root or a dangling creeper, troubles that could sabotage the GPLF's war and land them all in prison or before a firing squad.

Moving the treasure was a wise precaution, but it also amplified the danger of discovery. So far, only a handful of the GPLF's rank and file knew anything about the hoard of artifacts, much less where they were located. That was about to change, since Cruz had drafted the main body of their men as laborers to relocate the treasure. Soon, each man who donned a pack and humped the Mayan objects to their new, still undetermined home would share the secret.

The waiting game would begin, to see which one of them would crack.

It was impossible, Alvarez thought, for any ragtag group of men to safeguard such a secret. Even with the best intentions, some of them were bound to talk. One might try to impress his family, while yet another boasted to an old friend or a village whore. Small talk aside, there was a possibility that one or more of Cruz's men might try to steal some portion of the treasure. Call it simple greed or compensation for their long months in the jungle. Either way, it meant dissension, wasted energy, and execution if the thieves were caught.

Worse yet, if they escaped to spread the word that Cruz and Alvarez were sitting on a treasure that could lift whole provinces from grinding poverty and realize the wildest dreams of all concerned, how many hundreds, thousands, would come searching for the hoard, willing to kill or die for gold, silver and gems?

Alvarez scowled into the darkness.

It could be a living nightmare if they were forced to move incessantly and drag the treasure with them everywhere they went. He wasn't even sure the GPLF had enough men to transport the treasure in a single move. Alvarez visualized a day when every waking moment was devoted to the trove of ancient artifacts, their curse eclipsing everything the GPLF had been founded to accomplish.

It was hideous, but he could think of no alternative.

The treasure had revitalized their movement in its darkest hour, giving Cruz and Alvarez a new lease on their lives. Their first real hope of victory. They couldn't turn back, pretend that the discovery was never made. The ancient city had been breached, and it would someday be exposed to all the world. It made no sense for them to simply walk away, retreat into the bad old days when they had nothing and defeat loomed over them like Death's own shadow. Alvarez could never hint at such a possibility to Cruz.

But he might still suggest a compromise.

Why not?

They could evacuate sufficient treasure to support the movement for a year, five years—whatever they decided—without taking all of it and thus assuming an intolerable burden in the midst of wartime. Wealth could sometimes be a curse, particularly when it tipped the scales in tons, requiring days of miserable labor just to move the lot from one location to another.

Alvarez had joined the Guatemalan People's Liberation Front to *fight,* not to become a stevedore or watchman for a primitive museum. There had to be some way to convince Cruz. And if not…

He pressed on, brooding, following a train of thought as dark as any jungle night.

16

Carrie Travis paused for a moment to catch her breath. She heard Matt Cooper stop behind her. Up ahead, Luis Candera blazed their trail and Travis knew that she couldn't afford to lose sight of him. Cooper could probably find Candera in the jungle, but she didn't want to make him prove it. Couldn't stand for it to be her fault.

Cooper.

She wondered whether that was actually his name, but her questions in regard to their mysterious savior weren't limited to his identity. She thought about what he had said, his knowledge of her father's death coupled with stern denials of a quest for justice when he said he wasn't a cop.

That much was obvious. He was a soldier, clearly, but what kind? The sort she was familiar with traveled in squads or companies, sometimes battalions or divisions. They did not, as far as Travis knew, conduct one-man invasions of a foreign country, popping up to rescue damsels in distress or search for hidden treasure.

That made Cooper a fighting man, but not a soldier in the standard sense. Perhaps he was a spy, but everything she knew about the cloak-and-dagger world— which wasn't much— told Travis that a spy was unobtrusive, hard to spot, the kind of man or woman who could pass unnoticed in a crowd.

That definitely wasn't Cooper, with his gear and guns, athletic body, handsome face, or—

She caught herself, embarrassed like a schoolgirl in the first bloom of a crush. All Travis really felt for Cooper was a sense of gratitude shaded by mystery. They were embarked on an adventure, even though it frightened her and plainly worried him. It was exciting, and—

I'm too damned old for this, she thought.

Not literally, since her thirty-second birthday was a full five months away. With Cooper's help and ample luck, she just might live to see it.

What the small voice in her mind had meant to say was, "I'm too old for fantasies of tall dark strangers, daredevil adventures. Shit like that."

Yet, there she was, marching through trackless jungle with a native guide in front of her and the ultimate tall, dark stranger bringing up the rear. Watching *her* rear, for all she knew. Too bad she hadn't spent more hours in the gym before she caught the flight to Guatemala.

Stop it, she admonished herself.

Cooper hadn't snatched her from the clutches of a rebel army squad to get a date. He was a decent man—scary, but decent all the same, as far as she could tell—who couldn't leave two innocents to an uncertain fate in hostile hands.

And he was looking for Site X.

How weird was that? she thought. What kind of once-in-half-a-million-lifetimes bit of serendipity had caused their paths to cross just when she needed him?

Maybe it was just dumb luck.

Whatever, she concluded. She now had a second chance and didn't plan to waste it. If the price of vindicating her father's work, his very life, was helping Cooper find Site X, so be it. She would take her chances with the need-to-know commando, trusting in her own ability to find out more about his mission as they went along.

And if his orders involved some catastrophic damage to the ancient site, what then?

Don't sweat it, she told herself. If he was a savage, he'd have left you to the goons.

But she knew there were infinite degrees of savagery. If Cooper had been ordered to destroy Site X and thereby serve some greater good, she had no doubt that he would carry out those orders to the best of his ability. Unless she stopped him.

How?

She had no weapons, and she clearly couldn't best him in a hand-to-hand encounter. Even if Candera helped her, it would still be difficult, perhaps impossible. Travis supposed she might catch Cooper napping, find some way to overpower him before he woke and snapped her neck, but—

She didn't know his plans yet, had no reason to conspire against the man who'd saved her life and possibly her virtue.

She concentrated on the bare suggestion of a trail in front of her, focused on keeping pace with Candera and not making any more stupid mistakes. She could wait until she knew what Cooper intended for Site X.

Assuming that they ever found it.

And that the journey did not claim their lives.

BOLAN FOLLOWED Luis Candera's lead, the woman slogging on between them, but he didn't trust the guide completely. Every hour or so, he checked his GPS device to satisfy himself that they were still proceeding in a general northeasterly direction.

Based on her arguments and evident sincerity, he'd granted Travis one day in which to prove her case. If they still had nothing to show for it by nightfall, he was ready for Plan B. Ignoring anything she said and any thought of perils she might face, he would leave Travis and Candera to their own devices and strike off to find the rebel party led by Paco Alvarez. Site X might not be Alvarez's destination, but the snatch-and-grill scenario was still an active option.

And if Travis failed him, it would be the only game in town.

He worried that she might try something foolish, if and when they reached the site. Already, he could feel her gnawing on the thought that Cruz and Alvarez had killed her father. Would a craving for revenge subvert her scientific yearning for discovery and preservation of the ancient Mayan site? And what would happen if her better instincts clashed with Bolan's mission, if he had to blow Site X to keep its treasure out of rebel hands?

There'd been no way to prearrange assistance from the Guatemalan government. For starters, the locals never would have granted permission for Americans to invade their sovereign territory. Something might've been arranged through channels—with a payoff, diplomatic favors, maybe some assistance from the CIA—but those negotiations could've taken weeks or months, and Bolan didn't have that kind of time. Likewise, the Guatemalan government was riddled with corruption and there'd been no time to cultivate a trusted source inside the system. Any offers made from Stony Man Farm or Washington could have been relayed to the other side while Hal Brognola's plan was on the drawing board.

And having bypassed normal channels to begin his probe, Bolan could not rely on them for succor this late in the game. If he made contact with the army or the state security police, it would be *him* they hunted, shot or dumped in prison, while the GPLF took advantage of the sideshow to complete its looting of Site X.

Bolan had various half-baked scenarios in mind for the completion of his mission, but he couldn't follow through on any certain one until he reached their destination, took its measure and decided what was possible. So far, he didn't know Site X's size or how much treasure it contained, had no idea if there were any useful roads or waterways nearby for transportation of the hoard. He obviously couldn't shift the loot himself, even with Travis and Candera to assist him, but if he could summon outside help…

Bolan resisted the impulse to count his unhatched chickens, knowing that he couldn't count on Able Team or any other friendly faces in his present circumstances. Brognola had not dispatched him to retrieve the Mayan treasure, simply to ensure that Cruz and company received no further benefits from their discovery. With every forward step he took, that felt more like an order to destroy Site X.

That brought him back full-circle to the waiting game.

The smell of wood smoke reached his nostrils. Bolan stopped dead on the trail, saw Travis stop in front of him. He snapped his fingers at Luis Candera, saw the guide turn back to face him. Bolan brushed past Travis, met the Indian halfway. She moved in close behind him as he braced their guide.

"You want to tell me why we're heading for a village?" he inquired, stone-faced.

Candera smiled. "We need supplies and information," he replied. "These are my people. Do not fear."

Bolan put every ounce of grim reality into his eyes and voice as he responded. "If you're leading us into a trap," he said, "I'm not the one who needs to be afraid."

17

Tomas Aguirre enjoyed a peculiar love-hate relationship with the jungle. He hated its incessant rain, its suffocating heat, its vile leeches, mosquitoes and blood-sucking flies, its spiders, scorpions, venomous snakes and screeching monkeys, filthy water and disease. But he adored its hidden riches and the life-style they had granted him.

Aguirre was a scavenger, although when chatting up the ladies over drinks he commonly described himself as an explorer and adventurer. All the labels fit him well enough, in fact, since he had frequently explored backwater areas of Guatemala and surrounding countries, while surviving various adventures in the process. Over twenty years of fortune-hunting he'd been chased by natives, rebels and policemen. He'd canoed through rapids and been cast over a waterfall. He'd survived beatings, gunshots, a helicopter crash, a poisoned arrow and the bite of a bushmaster—all before the age of thirty-five.

And in the process, he had gotten rich.

Tomas Aguirre had the Devil's luck, an enemy—long since deceased—had once remarked. Aguirre, for his part, was never one to quibble over where his luck came from, as long as it ran true. And so far, it had served him well.

At least, until the past two days.

He'd made his greatest find, the score of any fortune hunter's lifetime, nearly two years earlier, while searching for an airplane full of drug money that had vanished while en route from Yucatán to Bogotá. The plane and money were still out there, somewhere, but Aguirre didn't need them anymore. Instead of greenbacks bundled up in duffel bags, he'd found Site X.

Of course, he hadn't coined the name. Tomas Aguirre didn't name his finds, much less give up his precious edge by advertising them. He simply memorized coordinates and marked his large-scale maps with pinpricks scarcely visible to naked eyes.

But if he'd been required to name his last and greatest find, Aguirre would've called it El Dorado. It was everything a rootless seeker after easy loot could hope for. That, and much, much more.

At first, he'd thought it was simply another ruined city of the ancients, not the first he'd found in twenty years and valuable only for the small reward he might receive from selling its coordinates to some museum or university. Still, he had been intrigued enough to spend the night among those ruins, barely glimpsed at dusk, and to explore the site more fully after sunrise the next day.

That day became a fevered week of prying into nooks and crannies, tombs and storerooms, swiftly cataloging riches that had stunned Aguirre, left him wondering if he was stricken with a fever that he didn't recognize and dying in a beautiful delirium.

But it was real.

And it was his.

But Aguirre couldn't shift the goods himself, and while he'd never stumbled onto anything this huge before, he recognized the need for maximum security. If he approached the government, he would be brushed off like a pesky gnat, his bounty confiscated by the state. Aguirre knew various dealers who could move the merchandise discreetly, but he couldn't shift the larger pieces from their hiding place alone and dared not deal with common criminals for fear of being shot and buried in a shallow grave as soon as he led them to the treasure.

His solution to the problem was a gamble, but it had paid off handsomely. Years earlier, while fitfully pursuing higher education, he had shared an economics class with Alejandro Cruz. Aguirre left the course at midterm with a failing grade, while Cruz stayed on and fumed over the crimes of wealthy men. Cruz went on to lead the Guatemalan People's Liberation Front, a group Aguirre recognized as long on zeal and always short of cash. The answer to his problem was simplicity itself. A devil's bargain with the GPLF ensured security for El Dorado while Aguirre took his share—albeit radically reduced from the ideal hundred percent—and basked in newfound luxury.

But now, after the better part of two years, it appeared that someone was attempting to derail his gravy train. Santos Medina had been rubbed out like a common thug, and Cruz was worried that Site X had been compromised. That brought Aguirre to his forced march through the stinking jungle over trails he did not recognize, moving toward the coordinates he knew by heart.

It pleased him not at all to march with Cruz's rebels, knowing that a chance encounter with a government patrol could send him to a mass grave or a stinking prison cell, but what choice did he have? Cruz needed him to rank the artifacts still waiting for them in the jungle, oversee their packing and removal to another site located God knew where. Refusal had not been an option.

Still, the good news was that they should reach Site X soon, with men and guns enough to fend off any challenge from the competition who had killed Medina. Once the treasures had been safely relocated, he could find another fence—or several, this time, to play it safe—and pick up where the flow of income had been rudely interrupted by Medina's murder.

It was simple.

Just like dying in the jungle, if he got too cocky and relaxed his guard.

Aguirre didn't plan to let that happen. He meant to enjoy a long life filled with luxury, fine food and luscious women who pretended to adore him. If that life required a bit of sacrifice, so be it. He would even join in spilling blood, if necessary.

Just as long as it belonged to someone else.

THE VILLAGE WASN'T LARGE, perhaps a dozen small thatched huts around a central fire pit, with a longhouse for communal gatherings set back among the trees. Bolan had smelled the fire but saw no sentries, yet the village was alerted when they reached it, its inhabitants turned out with weapons ranging from machetes to a rifle that was probably brand-new in World War I.

Despite their armament, the villagers did not seem hostile. On the contrary, in fact, their chief met Luis Candera with a toothy smile and rough, backslapping hug. The others eyed Bolan and Carrie Travis with suspicion clearly written on their faces, but they made no hostile moves. Bolan, in turn, took care to keep his hands well separated from his own hardware.

"This is my village," Candera said when the greetings in his native tongue had been completed. "No one will harm you here."

Bolan chose not to argue, though he didn't like the thought of Paco Alvarez and company discovering the village when their blood was up, still angry over having lost their hostages. The odds would be against these simple children of the forest, but he couldn't second-guess Candera if the guide was bent on leading trouble to his own doorstep.

Candera made the introductions, Bolan trying to remember names that often sounded like a burst of verbal static, clicks and chirps in place of vowels and consonants. Whatever dialect the villagers were using to communicate, it wasn't Spanish, and it definitely wasn't English. Travis tried to make a go of it, repeating each name as she heard it for the first time, but her efforts still produced giggles from children in the smallish crowd.

Bolan had counted twenty-seven people of all ages, with a handful left to go, when he was interrupted by Candera saying, "We are asked to share a meal and talk about the place you seek."

Bolan couldn't resist a glance at Carrie Travis, but he let her ask the question. "What? They know about Site X?"

Candera shrugged. "The forest is our mother, *señorita*. It keeps secrets, but they are discovered over time."

Standing with fists on hips, Travis addressed the guide as if he'd slapped her face. "Damn it, Luis! You knew where I could find it all along? Why didn't you just tell me?"

"*Señorita*, if you will recall, you never asked me where to find this place you call Site X. I am employed to help you find it and have done so. If your information was mistaken, I would have corrected you…but tactfully."

Candera's English had improved dramatically since entering the village—a phenomenon not lost on Bolan, who supposed the guide had grown adept at catering to tourists who were sometimes arrogant racists. Carrie Travis hadn't picked up on it yet, but she was getting there, the flush of anger leeching from her cheeks.

"So, you can lead us to the city?" she inquired.

Candera nodded. "As my cousin would have led your father, had they lived."

The final statement staggered Travis. Bolan was prepared to grab her arm in case she folded, but she pulled herself together and came back for more.

"You knew my father?"

"He stood where you are standing now," Candera said. "May I explain?"

"You'd better."

"First, something to drink?"

"No thank you. Please get on with it!"

"My people make their living from the forest," Candera said. "Hunting, fishing, growing what we can. Today, some of us live in Flores, but the forest still remains our home. When strangers like your father and yourself need guides, we show them what they want to see."

"For money," Travis said.

"Of course. Most of the strangers want to kill something and brag about it to their friends back home. A few shoot only photographs. A very few seek knowledge and would help the people they find here to have a better life."

"My father?" Travis sounded almost childlike.

"He hired my cousin Hector," Candera said, "looking for the Mayan city. Others had been there before him, looting, but I think your father truly wanted to preserve the ancient things."

"He did. He would have."

"Hector brought him here, to meet my people. They were going on to see the city next, but someone stopped them in the forest. Hector fought and died. We found him where he fell. The killers took your father. Only later did we learn what had become of him."

"You know who killed my father, then?" Travis asked.

"No one living saw their faces," Candera said in reply, "but some have seen the men who loot the city. I believe they are the same. Perhaps the men who held us earlier."

"And you've done nothing to prevent it?" Travis challenged.

"We are simple people, *señorita*," he replied.

Candera's eyes shifted to Dolan's face. "But with a fighting man to lead us, something might be done."

18

It irritated Alejandro Cruz that he should have to stop and rest his men, but logic told him that they could not march around the clock. He had already gained some time by pushing on through darkness, but the effort had cost two men missing from the ranks when it was light enough to watch them pass.

Deserters.

It was nothing new to Cruz, of course. Men joined the movement for whatever reason, some to stay and fight until the bitter end, while others battled private issues of their own. Some lost that struggle, others won it, but in either case the outcome of the private conflict might persuade a soldier that his time was better spent in other ways.

Cruz knew he should not blame them, yet he did. They had sworn oaths of loyalty to the movement and to him. He had no sympathy for traitors or fair-weather warriors who decided midway through their service that the struggle was too difficult, its cost too high.

Worse yet, when cowards fled they always took weapons, equipment and provisions with them, stealing from their comrades and the freedom struggle. Most of them had come to Cruz with nothing but the rags on their backs, then fled with rifles, ammunition, food—the very things his soldiers needed to survive.

He had no time to chase the two most recent traitors, but

Cruz knew their names and faces. He would not forget. Someday, if he encountered them while passing through a rural village or while walking down a city street, he would have his revenge.

Aguirre joined him, lowering himself onto the log that served Cruz as a bench. "This time tomorrow, we should be there," he observed.

"Good. First thing, we need to send off scouts in search of somewhere safe to hide the artifacts when we remove them," Cruz said.

"I've been giving that some thought," Aguirre said. "I may have a solution for you."

"Tell me where."

"We're climbing," Aguirre said. "Still not into mountains yet, but getting there. The city's flanked by peaks on either side, one thing that kept it hidden for so long. It's not that easy getting in and out, as you'll remember. As for aerial reconnaissance—"

"It's difficult, I understand. Get on with your idea," Cruz said.

Aguirre did not take offense. "The mountains all around the site are riddled," he explained, "with caves. I studied some of them before I found the city. Some are fairly large. It won't be easy, carrying some of the larger pieces uphill to the caves, but we have ropes and pulleys. When you need to take them out again, you use gravity."

"These caves," Cruz said. "Where are they, in relation to the site? How far away?"

"A mile or so on level ground," Aguirre said, "before we have to climb. That's to the west. Eastward, the nearest mountain is about two miles away."

"Who knows about these caves?" Cruz asked.

Aguirre shrugged. "I found no evidence that they were ever occupied, except by animals. There was a village in the area, but I—"

"What village?" Cruz demanded.

Yet another shrug. "I didn't get a name," Aguirre said. "I

didn't pay a visit. Just some village in the jungle. Maybe Indians."

"What if they know about the caves?"

"As I already said, there was no evidence—"

"We should not take the chance," Cruz said.

"Okay, no caves. I'll try to think of something else, but—"

"You mistake me, Tomas. I think we *should* use the caves."

"But you just said—"

"I said we must not take a chance that anyone knows where they are."

"And since we can't be sure—"

"We make sure," Cruz suggested.

"And how do we do that?"

Cruz answered with a question of his own. "How long do you suppose it will take to move the treasure, with the men we have?"

Aguirre pondered that for several moments, then replied, "To do a proper job and get it all stored in the caves, at least a week. It could be more."

"And if we had more hands?"

"Then, obviously, it would be a quicker job."

"It's settled, then."

"What's settled?" Aguirre asked.

"We shall ask the local villagers to help us," Cruz replied.

"What makes you think they'll go along with it?"

Smiling, Cruz remarked, "I have a talent for persuasion."

"I'm against it," Aguirre said. "First, you're worried they may know about the caves, and now you want their help storing the artifacts inside them. If they didn't know about the caves before, they will when we get done. And they'll know where to go whenever they need trinkets they can sell for pocket money."

"But they won't," Cruz said. "I promise you."

"How's that?"

"They'll be in no condition to steal anything from us."

It took another heartbeat, but Aguirre got the message. Solemnly, he nodded, staring at his boots. "I see. But Alejandro—"

"I know what you want to say, Tomas. We're fighting for the people, and I plan to kill them. It's a necessary sacrifice. I can't allow the movement to be undermined. I'm pledged to see it through."

"Of course." Aguirre's answer was subdued, almost a whisper.

"I have shocked you, Tomas. Did you think that this was all a game? Men playing soldier in the forest for their own amusement?"

"No, of course not. But in the past you've only killed soldiers."

Cruz frowned at that but did not bother to correct Aguirre. There was nothing to be gained by trampling all of his illusions in a single afternoon. Instead, Cruz said, "Don't let it worry you, Tomas. The blood is on my hands, not yours."

"I'm not sure where to find the village, anyway," Aguirre said.

"Don't worry," Cruz replied, reaching for his sat phone. "Paco has a gift for finding what is lost."

BOLAN WASN'T THRILLED with the new plan, but argument seemed fruitless. If he turned down the offer, refused to play along, the villagers would make a stab at it without him and they'd surely reach the Mayan city first, while he was left to carry on without a guide.

He'd tried to draw the line at letting Carrie Travis tag along, but she'd been adamant about accompanying them and since Candera's people held her late father in such esteem, rejecting Travis had the same effect as spurning all of them.

The deal was bound to mean civilians in the line of fire, assuming that the GPLF war party was heading for Site X. Bolan couldn't be sure of that, but they were moving in the right direction, and Candera's chief confirmed that armed guerrilla parties visited the site at bimonthly intervals.

Tapping the till, Bolan thought. *Cashing in.*

After a filling meal of stew, the villagers who had been picked to join Bolan packed their meager gear and turned out, ready for a march into the dusk. The Executioner reviewed their motley arsenal: a Springfield Model 1903 rifle, two old shotguns—one a double-barrel, one pump-action—plus a mix of bows, blowguns, machetes, and a double-headed ax with rust spots on its blades. Bolan felt as if he was marching to battle through a time warp.

But there might not be a battle. There was still a chance, however slight, that Paco Alvarez and his guerrillas might be heading somewhere else. They might bypass Site X this time, and come again some other day. By that time, Bolan hoped, he would have placed the Mayan treasure well beyond their reach.

Travis had armed herself for combat with a borrowed butcher knife, tucked through her belt at a rakish angle to keep it from stabbing her if she sat down. Bolan might have smiled at the look of grim determination on her face, if the stakes had been anything short of life or death.

"We should be going while the light remains," Candera said.

"You're right."

Standing in the village square, Bolan reviewed his troops one last time. Candera had recruited seven other men, ranging in age from twenty-something to the ax man in his early fifties. Travis made it ten in all, perhaps the strangest group Bolan had ever ventured out with to the hellgrounds.

Up against how many guns? Bolan had counted a dozen men with Alvarez, which wouldn't be the worst odds he had ever faced. After he factored in the natives' knowledge of the terrain, their woodcraft and their hunting skills, Bolan supposed they might be points ahead.

But Travis said that Alvarez was on his way to meet someone. He'd told her so, in no uncertain terms, and it made no sense to assume that he was marching through the jungle toward a rendezvous with one lone man. If Alvarez was heading toward Site X, the odds were good that he expected company.

My doing, Bolan thought, thinking about Santos Medina and the bloody work he'd done in Guatemala City. It had likely rattled Alejandro Cruz and set him thinking, scheming to protect his stash.

So be it.

Bolan had been hoping for a chance to rattle Cruz and company. He had apparently succeeded, even though it might have repercussions he had not anticipated. Facing danger was his job, but what about the others? What would he do if they were killed or maimed?

I'll live with it, he told himself, and fell into the line of march, trailing Candera from the village toward their target.

Toward Site X.

PACO ALVAREZ WAS slapping at mosquitoes when the sat phone trembled in his pocket. He'd turned off the ringer for security's sake, but left the vibe mode engaged on the chance that Cruz might try to reach him while he was en route to the ruined city.

He listened to the order and acknowledged it, having no choice in that regard. When Cruz had finished speaking, Alvarez had a chance to tell him what had happened with the woman and her Indian but he kept it to himself.

Why aggravate a situation that was already confused? Why worry Cruz when he had so many other pressing matters on his mind?

Why put my own head in a noose? Alvarez thought, and spit into the ferns along the left side of the narrow trail.

He whistled for his men to stop, sent one to call the scouts back and stood waiting until all of them were present. Some knew he'd received a call and word had spread quickly. All of them watched Alvarez with tense, expectant faces.

"We have new orders," he informed them. "Commander

Cruz requires us to locate a village. He's given me directions, but I've never seen the place myself. Do any of you come from this part of the country? Have you heard of any villages near our destination?"

Long silence stretched between them, then a young guerrilla with a pitiful mustache and acne scars lifted a cautious hand. *"Jefe?"*

"If you have information, make it known," Alvarez said.

"There is a village that way," the young man said, pointing vaguely in the general direction they'd been traveling.

"You've seen it?" Alvarez inquired.

"Yes, sir. Once."

"Between two rivers, with a small mountain beyond?"

A jerky nod. "Yes, sir."

"Tell me about the people.

"They are…hostile."

"What makes you believe that?"

"They accused me of…some things…and tried to kill me. I was lucky to escape."

Lucky for all of us, Alvarez thought. "How big a village was it?"

"Small," the soldier said. "No more than ten or fifteen houses."

"Does it have a name?"

"None that I ever heard, sir."

"But you could find it," Alvarez suggested.

"Sir, I…"

"Assuming that your life depended on it?"

"Yes."

"Good. That's settled, then. You'll lead us to the village. Introduce us to your friends."

Alvarez lost his smile a heartbeat later, barking at his troops, "Fall in! We're wasting time!"

It was a strange sensation, marching off to war against a village he had never seen, or even heard of until moments earlier. Granted, he ambushed strangers every other week, but those were soldiers paid to hunt him down and make his life a misery. The people he was hunting now were simply people, of the sort the Guatemalan People's Liberation Front was pledged to liberate.

Still, Alvarez would do as he was told.

Cruz always had his reasons, never gave an order without thinking through the problems it might cause. Besides, he hadn't ordered Alvarez to *kill* the villagers. He simply was to enlist their aid in shifting treasure from the ancient Mayan city. He supposed that Cruz would pay them something for their labor when the job was done.

Or maybe not.

The whole diversion had a strange, unsettling feel about it. Alvarez could understand Cruz suddenly deciding that they needed extra hands to move the artifacts. It was a simple oversight that anyone could make. But dragging people from their homes at gunpoint would destroy whatever goodwill the rebels had accumulated in the area, perhaps forever.

Only if the word gets out, a small voice in his head replied.

That was the key, then, he decided. They were marching on a village unfamiliar to him, where his men except for one—were seemingly unknown. The GPLF had no reputation to destroy among the nameless town's inhabitants, beyond whatever they had heard by word of mouth. As for their own experience, it only hurt the cause if it was shared with others.

And he reckoned that Cruz would not allow that.

So it was more than captive labor, then. The plan made perfect sense to Alvarez. They couldn't kidnap locals, force the lot of them to work against their will, then leave them with their knowledge of a treasure that would make them rich beyond their wildest, fevered dreams. If they were normal, if they held a grudge like anybody else on Earth, they would retaliate by cleaning out the hoard as soon as they were able to.

Unless someone prevented it.

Alvarez supposed that part would be his job, as well. He didn't want it, but unless he led a mutiny there was no way around it. He could either do as he was told or put his own head on the chopping block.

And finally, what difference did it make to Alvarez? He'd already killed dozens, scores of people in the movement's name. Soldiers had families and souls. How different were peasants from the forest, when he put the thing under a microscope?

How different am I? he wondered, and found no answer that relieved his mind.

Perhaps the place would be deserted when they found it. Maybe it was market day, and everyone had gone off to another village, safe beyond his reach. Or maybe they had simply pulled up stakes and moved away. Perhaps he'd find them too well armed to be intimidated.

Possibly.

And if he had to kill them, Alvarez would find a way to live with it.

He always did.

19

A mile or so outside the nameless village, Carrie Travis started wondering if she had lost her mind. What had possessed her to insist that she accompany Matt Cooper and a tiny group of total strangers to confront a trained guerrilla army in the ruins of an ancient Mayan city? Was it some kind of bizarre memorial to all her father's work, or had she simply gone insane?

Their scheme was madness. She could hardly doubt that much. Ten people in her party, only four of them with guns, against a paramilitary force of unknown size, its members all accomplished killers who'd survived a long war of attrition with the Guatemalan army.

Perfect.

And the best that she could do, in terms of weaponry, had been a borrowed butcher knife. It was pathetic, verging on ridiculous. Travis could barely hack through ferns and vines to blaze a trail, much less charge into battle against gunmen armed with military weapons.

This is where you die, she thought. Like Dad.

That hadn't been the plan, of course. She'd given only passing thought to danger when she learned about her father's death. The pressing need was to do something, prod the negligent authorities into doing their jobs and arresting the killers. Failing that—and fail she had—Travis was determined to retrace her father's steps, see what he'd seen and carry on to realize his dream.

But it had turned into a nightmare with no exit, and her own big mouth had launched her on another jungle journey that could only be a death march in the end. What hope did any of them have against their enemies?

The group that had abducted her was marching toward a rendezvous with reinforcements. Cooper seemed to think that march would take them to Site X, but Travis had begun to hope that he was wrong. Her only chance of visiting the Mayan city and surviving to report the find resided in the possibility of the guerrillas going somewhere else.

Forget it, she thought. The way my luck's been running, that's exactly where they're going. All two thousand of them, or whatever it turned out to be.

She was as good as dead, and suddenly reminded that she wanted very much to live.

Cooper, for his part, didn't seem tremendously concerned about their prospects. He was stoic to a fault, plodding along as if he could've marched for days on end without a breather, going on forever like a deadly version of the Energizer Bunny.

Travis hoped that he was deadly, anyway.

So far, she'd only seen him cut a tent when nobody was looking, but he carried guns and God knew what else, seeming ready for whatever came his way. Travis had tried in vain to tap into his confidence, or even the grim resignation of Candera's fellow villagers, but none of it was working for her.

She was scared. That was the bottom line.

Cooper had wanted her to stay behind, had argued for it, but she'd worn him down with talk about her knowledge of the Mayans and of Site X. She thought he'd given in at last to shut her up and keep from wasting any more time, perhaps hoping she'd change her mind and run back to the shelter of the village when they'd marched a while into the rain forest at dusk.

And Travis was embarrassed that she longed to do exactly that.

Two things kept her from running at the moment—stubborn pride and an oppressive certainty that she'd be lost before she walked a quarter of a mile alone.

She didn't want to die, but if she had to choose a method from the options presently available, she'd stick with Cooper's team and risk a bullet, rather than embarking on a solo jungle trek that might end with a snakebite, in a jaguar's jaws or quicksand.

She'd have traded her diplomas for a one-way ticket to the States, just then—or would she?

There was still the lure of her father's dream, his grand obsession. It was leading Travis to her death, as it had him, but now that she was trapped with no way out, at least she had a chance to make the most of it.

At least she'd see Site X.

Unless they met the GPLF first and all of them were killed.

Despondent, blinking back a surge of angry tears, she followed Cooper through the forest while night came on along behind them, spreading silent, pitch-black wings.

BOLAN HAD BEEN PREPARED to march on through the night, but when Luis Candera called a halt for darkness he agreed. The natives wouldn't press on in defiance of Candera's order, even if he urged them to, and Carrie Travis had the look of someone verging on exhaustion. As for Bolan, he was ready to proceed but didn't know the way.

Checkmate.

They camped without a fire, ate some kind of dried meat and some fruit they had picked along the way. Bolan had eaten worse—had gone without, in fact, from time to time—and he was satisfied.

Candera posted lookouts, scheduled shifts, but it was still too early for the team to sleep. Travis remained awake by sheer determination, as if fearing that a failure to participate would cause her to be stricken from the team.

"We never knew the city could be so important," Candera said, sitting with his back against a tree, a cold pipe clenched between his teeth. "We normally avoid it."

"What, no curiosity?" Travis asked.

"Those who built it were our ancestors," Candera said. "We know their stories. We don't need to see their bones."

"It isn't that," she said. "Not *only* that, I mean. We need to learn about the past, discoveries as well as the mistakes, to help us find our way."

"Sounds good in theory," Bolan interjected, "but we've had museums and libraries for centuries and people haven't changed. Not for the better, anyway."

"You're quite the cynic," Travis said.

"I think of it as realism, based on personal experience," Bolan replied.

"I guess you lead a grim life."

"It's been said," he admitted.

"I suppose I'm thankful that I don't know what that's like," Travis said.

"But you're here," Bolan reminded her, "chasing a dead man's dream that may kill *you*."

She stiffened but controlled herself. "I don't know how things were between you and your parents," Travis said. "My mother died when I was six years old. I hardly recognize her photos now. But I revered my father, everything he did. I grew up sharing his enthusiasms and his aspirations. He was a professor, so I had to be one. Archaeology, of course. I guess you find that all ridiculous."

"I wouldn't say ridiculous," Bolan replied. "And certainly it's not unique. Millions of people join the family business, whether it's carpentry or medicine, the Army or the law."

"It's not just that," Travis said. "Ever since he started looking for Site X, my father had a new vitality, new passion in his life. It almost made him young again."

"It killed him, Carrie."

"No. Men killed him, Cooper. And before they did, he lived. How many people in your personal experience can say the same?"

"A few," he said. The ones who mattered, anyway.

"And you? Have *you* lived? Seen the things you hoped to see when you were younger? Done the things you dreamed of doing?"

"I've seen the world," he answered, "but you won't find most of what I've seen in any guidebook. As for childhood dreams, I don't recall."

She studied Bolan's face, her own partly concealed by shadows. "I feel sorry for you, Cooper."

"Hold that thought," he said. "I may feel sorry for myself tomorrow, or the next day. We can be sorry together."

"What about Site X?" she asked him.

"What about it?"

"I get that you're the strong and silent type," she said, "but there's something happening inside that head of yours. You've got a plan you're keeping from the rest of us."

"Not really."

"No?"

He bit the bullet. "Look, I've told you why I'm here."

"To keep the Mayan treasure out of rebel hands. But how?"

"By any means available," Bolan said.

"You'd destroy the city, just to make a point? For politics?"

"I don't know if that's possible," he told her honestly. "I haven't seen the place. It might require an air strike, and I don't have that facility."

"Thank God!"

"I'd save the prayers, if I were you," Bolan said. "There's a good chance that you may be spending time with Paco Alvarez again, before too long. If you've got some divine intervention on tap, you could make good use of it then. But for now, you ought to get some sleep."

20

Paco Alvarez allowed his men to sleep in shifts, with four guards posted at a time. He woke them at the first gray light of dawn. Alvarez himself had slept but little, trying it after the sentries on the first shift took their posts. But every hour found him wide awake once more, rising to check the guards, make sure they were alert and in their proper places.

The loss of sleep did not bother him. Alvarez had long since given up on anything resembling a routine. He often stayed awake all night, on ambush duty or patrol, and made up for it when he could. There would be no rest for him this day, though, nor probably the next.

When his men had finished with their meager breakfast, packed their things and fallen into line, he faced them and explained their orders for the day. He told them of the village, how the labor of its people was required to help the movement, and resistance could not be permitted. Alvarez caught several men frowning, marking them as ones to watch during the march and overnight. He was prepared to execute the first man he caught trying to desert but hoped it wouldn't come to that. If it began to fall apart, there would be hell to pay.

He asked for questions, a deviation from his normal method of command, but none was raised. He guessed most of the men would do as they were told, and none would challenge him directly. Those who fled the GPLF's ranks did not announce their reasons, merely slipping off into the jungle like the cowards that they were.

So be it. He would watch them all and show no mercy to any who betrayed him.

His new guide had reported that the village was approximately four miles distant from their camp. Fearing the possibility of traps and lookouts, Alvarez had not tried to approach it after nightfall, barring even scouts from going on to count the settlement's inhabitants. He meant to take his chances in the daylight, when it was more difficult for fugitives to slip away unseen.

While he had never captured slaves before, the method should be similar to any other hostage situation. First, impress the hostages with force, making it clear that punishment awaited any disobedience. In the event of physical resistance, crush it ruthlessly. Make an example of the worst offenders and the rest would soon fall into line.

And if they still refused…then, what?

He had already come to terms with the idea that he would have to execute the villagers when they had finished serving Cruz. Having accepted that, it would be no more difficult to slaughter them a day or two ahead of schedule—but that would constitute a breach of orders and would leave him short of workers when he reached the Mayan city.

Kill a few, then, if we have to, he decided. Just a few, and take the rest.

He'd spent a good part of the night thinking of children, what to do with them. They made the best of hostages—a blade pressed to a son or daughter's throat would normally induce compliance from the parents—but the smaller ones would have no value when the heavy work began.

No matter. He would hand that problem off to Cruz upon delivery. He had to shoulder some responsibility for the activities he set in motion, after all.

Alvarez knew there might be trouble with the men when

it was time to get rid of the villagers. Abducting them and forcing them to work was one thing, justified in theory by the movement's pressing need. Some might refuse an order to annihilate the hostages, but Alvarez did not believe it would provoke a general mutiny. His men had seen and done too much already, crossed the bloody line too many times to stand back and pretend that they were civilized.

Still, every soldier had a breaking point, some line he could not—would not—cross. Guerrilla warfare tested boundaries, but no commander truly knew when one or more of his soldiers might fail him. It was a risk that no plan could avert, no amount of concern lay to rest.

Two hours on the jungle trail, and Alvarez was just about to call a halt for rest when the point man returned, looking winded and nervous. "The village," he announced. "I have found it."

Alvarez signaled a halt to the column. "Show me," he commanded.

"Another quarter mile."

Alvarez called three men to join him. One, his most trusted sergeant, would remain behind and watch the rest while he was gone. The others bobbed their heads when ordered to accompany him and the scout.

"All right," he told the runner who had found the village. "Lead the way."

It seemed to take forever, though Alvarez knew it was only a matter of ten or fifteen minutes. They moved with extra care, unwilling to alert their prey, though Alvarez assumed the scout had checked for sentries prior to doubling back. They met no booby traps along the way and reached a hidden vantage point outside the village.

He scanned the tiny settlement, breathed in its wood smoke, listened to its people as they went about their morning business. There were no dogs visible, and none of the inhabitants that Alvarez could see were armed with anything more dangerous than bolo knives. He did not underestimate a blade in able hands, but reckoned that his men could hold their own with M-16s.

He counted twenty-seven people of all ages and assumed there had to be more inside the huts, or off on work details. He'd have to check that, making sure that none was left behind to track him and discover where the rest had gone.

Turning to the pair of soldiers who had come with him, he told one of them, "Go and fetch the rest. Be sure they understand that there must be no noise of any kind."

"Yes, sir."

"Go now."

The soldier bowed his head, then turned and vanished in a moment, moving back the way they'd come. Crouching beside the others, Alvarez clung to his rifle, waiting for his reinforcements to arrive.

BOLAN WAS NOT PREPARED for his first vision of Site X. One moment, he was slogging through the jungle with Luis Candera in the lead; the next, he halted on Candera's signal, then edged slowly forward with the Steyr AUG at the ready.

But it was not an enemy Candera wanted him to see.

It was a piece of history.

Seeing the ruins, Bolan understood how they had managed to lie undiscovered for so long. The jungle had reclaimed them. Vines and creepers, left unchecked for centuries, had covered every hand-carved surface, while moss grew underneath in colors nearly matching Bolan's camouflage fatigues. Wild grass had sprouted from the countless cracks in paving stones and steps, on roofs and ledges, giving everything a vaguely hairy look. Between the major buildings—and, in once case, from the very heart of one—great trees had sprouted, taken root and grown to towering maturity.

Bolan supposed that Site X had to have been invisible from any aerial perspective. Even hikers on the ground might take it for a field of boulders cast up by some prehistoric cataclysm. Only an incisive second look revealed the straight lines seldom found in nature, drawing the observer closer to pick out the features obviously wrought by human hands.

Bolan surveyed the site as best he could, scanning from left to right, gauging preliminary measurements. It was beyond what he'd expected, so much more than just a temple planted in the middle of a wilderness. It was the ruin of a city, without question, and he didn't have enough explosives to raze a quarter of it, much less everything he saw—or what remained as yet unseen.

An elbow jostled Bolan as Carrie Travis moved up to glimpse her father's dream made real in stone and mortar, standing finally revealed. "Dear God!" she gasped, and when he looked at her, Bolan saw bright tears streaming down her cheeks.

She started forward, but he caught her arm and drew her sharply back. "Not yet," he warned. "We need to check it out."

"That's what I had in mind," she said, shaking his hand away.

"For traps," Bolan explained.

"They'd be *inside* the buildings," Travis told him. "Mayan's didn't booby-trap their streets."

"It wasn't Mayans that I had in mind," Bolan replied.

That wiped the first flush of excitement from her face but left her fairly trembling with nervous energy, as if instead of marching through the rain forest for most of three days straight she'd only beamed in from her office at the university, confronted with a thousand things she had to do immediately.

"You think they're here already?" she asked Bolan. "Waiting for us?"

"I won't know until we have a careful look around the place."

"But after all this time—"

"This city's waited for a thousand years," Bolan reminded her. "It isn't going anywhere."

"He's right," Candera said. "Even if evil men are behind us, there will still be snakes and scorpions."

"I hear you. Easy does it. But how long are we supposed to stand here staring at it, without going any closer?" Travis asked.

Bolan almost smiled at her enthusiasm, but he caught himself in time. "You ought to wait here until someone comes and tells you it's all clear," he replied.

She got his message and it made her bristle. "Oh, no! If you think I'm going to stand back and wait while all of you go traipsing through the city, you are seriously mental."

Bolan rounded on her, grim-faced. "Listen," he said. "Candera's people know the forest, and I know guerrilla warfare. You know rocks and bones. We're not exploring, cracking any tombs, or making any claims. If trouble's waiting for us in there, you are *not* equipped to handle it. And I can't sacrifice a man to babysit right now. Give me your word that you'll stay here until you're called, or we'll tie you to a tree."

"You wouldn't dare!" she fumed.

"Luis, do we have rope?"

Candera smiled and answered, *"Sí, señor."*

Travis glared at them through a film of angry tears, then took a slow step back. "All right," she said at last. "But I warn you, don't try to open any doors or windows. If you find a door already open, do not go inside without me. I know this part, and we don't have the equipment to extract you if you run into a trap or cause a cave-in."

"Right," Bolan replied. "Agreed."

He turned next to their guide. "Luis, your men know what they're looking for. I'm less concerned with bats and snakes right now than with an ambush. If they spot someone, don't take him out until we talk about it and make sure we've got them all."

Aghast, Travis stepped forward, interrupting him. "What do you mean, 'don't take them out'? You plan to start a war in these historic ruins?"

"That's not up to me," Bolan replied. "If Alvarez and his guerrillas find us here, we've got a war. Case closed. The only question is who comes out on top."

MOST OF THE VILLAGERS came out to meet them, though a handful—mainly children—peered from doorways, watching Paco Alvarez and his assembled troops. The chief of the village was a sixty-something character with hair as white as egret's feathers dangling to his shoulders. He was leaning on some kind of walking stick that tapered to a point. Not quite a spear, but Alvarez resolved to keep his distance.

"What brings you to our village, stranger?" asked the headman.

"We are from the Guatemalan People's Liberation Front, and we are here to help you," Alvarez replied.

"Too late," the old man told him, with a crooked smile. "We are already liberated."

"You may think so, Grandfather, but there are better days ahead, when we depose the junta."

"Better days than these?" The headman feigned surprise.

"Much better. You can help us to achieve them," Alvarez said.

The old man lost his smile. "We do not mix in politics. The government leaves us alone, and we return the favor. So, you see—"

"I am afraid I must insist," Alvarez said.

"On what?"

"Your help, as I already said."

"Your men are hungry? Thirsty? I suppose that we can spare a little food, perhaps some beer. We have no weapons such as yours. No ammunition. We—"

"I don't require your food," Alvarez said. "I need you—all of you—to help me with a task of critical importance to the movement."

"What task?" the chief asked.

"There are certain objects we must move from one location to another," Alvarez stated. "It is simple work but needs more hands than we possess."

"You should recruit more men."

"This isn't battle, and we have no time. Your help is urgently required."

"Alas," the headman answered, "we have too much work already, for ourselves. Perhaps another time."

"There is no other time," Alvarez said. He raised his M-16, prepared to fire. The other guns came up with his. "You're coming with us now."

"Where would you take us?" the village elder asked.

"You may recognize it when we get there," Alvarez replied. "Now gather all your people. Quickly!"

The headman turned slowly, surveying faces, then returned his gaze to Alvarez. "This *is* all of us."

"No one cutting wood or fetching water?" Alvarez inquired. "No young men hunting? Fishing? It seems very strange to me."

"We are a small community," the headman told him. "Young ones go away as soon as they are able. Who can blame them, eh?"

"I think you're lying, old man."

"You seek aid and then insult me? This is not how things are done."

"Let me explain how things are done," Alvarez said. "You have one final chance to tell the truth and gather every member of this village here, to me. Send runners if you must. I will be generous. You have two hours to retrieve all stragglers from the forest. If the runners don't return or come back empty-handed, I'll shoot one of you for each of them. The small ones first, I think, since they're too weak to be much help at heavy work."

The villagers were muttering, but they made no aggressive move against the automatic rifles. Finally, the headman answered, "You are clever. I shall send the runners, as you say."

"No children," Alvarez warned him. "They stay here with us."

"As you command," the old man said.

Three men were chosen from the small crowd and dispatched toward different compass points. In parting, all of them spared hateful glances for the strangers in their midst.

Alvarez expected nothing less. He was the enemy. It made him feel uneasy, almost sickly, but he would obey his orders to the bitter end.

This time, at least.

Selecting three of his guerrillas, Alvarez commanded them to search the village, probing every hut and scouring the longhouse, beating bushes all around the settlement's perimeter. They flushed out two children and a woman with an infant in her arms, bringing the total of his hostages to thirty with three runners at large.

His soldiers were outnumbered, but Alvarez was not concerned. The search had revealed no weapons of any consequence, a few machetes and other chopping tools, left where they were beyond the reach of his collected prisoners. He did not think the villagers were desperate enough to rush his men, and he was certain that they could not stand before his automatic weapons.

He knew he would have to watch them closely on the trek to reach the treasure site, however. Any one of them could slip away and lose his soldiers in the jungle, given half a chance. But Alvarez meant to deliver each and every one of them as ordered. Let their fate and any guilt accruing from it rest squarely on Alejandro Cruz's shoulders.

Paco Alvarez was fighting for a sacred cause he loved.

All things were fair in love and war.

21

Sometimes, when he was marching through the jungle, Alejandro Cruz imagined that it had expanded to consume the world. It seemed to him as if there was no end to steaming vegetation, brilliant birds and monkeys screeching in the canopy far overhead, odd shafts of sunlight lancing through the constant twilight gloom. Sometimes that feeling helped him to relax.

And other times it nearly drove him mad.

Cruz knew exactly how long they'd been marching, could have timed it to the minute with his wristwatch, or he could've gone back to the moment when Aguirre reached his former base camp and they hatched their plan to foil his latest unknown enemies. Details did not escape him, but at times like this they grated on his nerves like fingernails dragged over slate.

They had been making decent progress. There were no patrols to intercept them, no great obstacles they were unable to surmount. By Cruz's estimate they were a bit ahead of schedule, but it didn't help. He still chafed with his need to see the ancient city, stand among its ruins one more time—and pick it clean while he still had the chance.

Historians might curse him, he thought, but they'd never had to struggle for their very lives against a ruthless government that stifled all dissent and smothered every hope of change. In theory, Cruz agreed with those who would preserve his nation's treasures for the benefit of generations yet unborn.

But academics lived in ivory towers, high above the toil and stench of daily life. To them, it was enough to brand a place or object as *historic* and declare that it should never be molested under any circumstances. What they failed to realize was that tomorrow's history was being made today, by men and women fighting for their lives, sometimes without a peso to their names.

So let them curse him, when they found out what he'd done. It would be when, Cruz thought, not if, since someone had been wise enough to track Santos Medina. The thought that haunted Cruz was that he might already be too late.

He wondered if Medina's death had been the last act of the play, and not the first. Suppose he reached the ruined city and discovered that its treasure had been swept away? What then?

In that case, Cruz supposed he'd find his enemies waiting, or at least some sign to help him trace them. It might be too late to salvage the remaining artifacts, but he could still hope for revenge.

Cruz had never been an optimist. He saw the glass as half-empty, with a leak below the waterline. He always expected the worst. A doctor had suggested medication for his black moods, during Cruz's second year of college, but he'd never filled the prescription. Life had taught him to expect adversity, and he saw nothing to be gained from sedatives.

Cruz knew he was unique among the revolutionary fighters of his homeland. All of them were ruthless and pragmatic, but they acted for the most part from a sense of hopefulness, albeit battered, bloodied and forlorn. They spoke and sang of liberty, wept at funerals, but greeted each new dawn with hope that this might be The Day.

Cruz mouthed the same slogans, struck the same poses, but he fought because resistance was the only thing he had. His family was dead to him, their station in society a shame that he could only wash away with blood. In his case, clinical depression had been elevated to the status of political philosophy.

And who could say that he was wrong?

Taking a slogan from the hated gringos, Cruz was fond of saying, "If it works, don't fix it."

But his private army wouldn't work—wouldn't survive—if it was starved, stripped of equipment and supplies. With that in mind, he had to salvage any remnants of the Mayan treasure for himself and for his men, at any cost. Failing that, he had to visit punishment upon enemies.

Tomas Aguirre approached, falling back along the line of march from his position near the point. His khaki shirt and pants were soaked with sweat and the sporadic rain that failed to provide relief from jungle heat.

"The scouts are looking for a place to camp," he said.

"Too early," Cruz replied.

"It's almost dark," the treasure hunter said.

And so it was. Cruz glowered at the shadows that would steal more precious time, perhaps allow his enemies the period of grace they needed to complete their looting of Site X. It galled him, but if he commanded that his men march on through darkness, more would almost certainly desert him

"All right," Cruz said at last. "We camp. How long tomorrow?"

"Noon, I think," Aguirre said. "It shouldn't be much later."

"Make it earlier," Cruz said. "We start at dawn."

"I NEVER REALIZED that it would be so big," Carrie Travis said, moving through the ruins of Site X at Bolan's side. "Maybe a temple with a reliquary. But a whole city!"

"Wasn't this your father's dream?" he asked.

"The truth is," she replied, "I thought he might be going overboard."

"And yet you came."

"I had to find out for myself."

It hadn't taken long to sweep the site for snipers, leaving the Executioner satisfied that any traps awaiting them had been prepared centuries before his birth. There were no mines, no trip wires fastened to grenades, but Travis hadn't taken long to locate evidence of human trespassers.

"Damn it, another one," she said, moving from Bolan's side to stand before an opening in a hillside. The cave's mouth was a yawning doorway, hacked and blasted open on the north side of a vine-encrusted mound that proved to be a stony pyramid.

"Bastards!" she said. "That's three, so far. I need to get inside and see what's left, find out what damage has been done."

"It's nearly dark," Bolan reminded her. "We can't afford to show a light where anyone could see it, coming through the jungle."

"But—"

"It's also twice as dangerous to poke around these ruins after nightfall," Bolan said. "I don't need a degree in archaeology to know that."

"I know. You're right," she said reluctantly. "You know the feeling, though. I'm sure of it. Working so long and hard for something that you can't wait any longer when it's there, within your reach?"

He knew the feeling, right enough.

And he had seen men die because of it.

"Tomorrow you can take one of Candera's people with you and explore the ruins to your heart's content," he said. And as he spoke, a small voice in his head added, *Unless someone drops in to pay a visit and we're busy fighting for our lives.*

She studied Bolan's face in twilight, asking, "So, now that you've seen it, what's the plan?"

"I'm not sure yet," he said. "Like you, I thought it would be smaller."

"Easier to blow it up that way, I guess."

"I have to look at all the options," he replied.

"To keep the reds or blacks or whoever it is this week from cashing in," she said.

"To keep it out of the wrong hands. Correct."

"But don't you see? The only *right* hands are the scientists and scholars who can study it, preserve it for the people."

"Or," Bolan replied, "we could eliminate the middlemen and simply let the people have it."

"You mean let them *loot* it!"

"I was thinking more of visits under supervision," Bolan said.

"Like what? A Mayan theme park?"

Bolan shrugged. "You're right about this being history. In fact, it's Guatemalan history. How many locals do you think will ever see the articles you write when you get back to Princeton or wherever?"

If she made it back.

"You're right again," she said. "I doubt if anyone will read about it, but a handful of professors and historians. That's not the point."

"What is?" Bolan inquired.

"We have an opportunity to safeguard something from the past, to find out where we came from."

"Where *they* came from," he corrected her.

"In any case. I know you understand what I'm trying to say."

He nodded. "Sure I do. And I agree with you, in principle. If we were living in Utopia, the very best thing you could do is set this place aside for study, maybe make it a museum. But the reality of life in Guatemala is that forty-five percent of all the country's people are illiterate. The infant mortality rate is forty-five per one thousand births, versus seven per one thousand in the States. The country's gross domestic is forty-eight billion dollars per year, but the average laborer doesn't clear four thousand. Peasants in the countryside are lucky to see half of that."

She frowned. "Your point being what? That we should hand out priceless artifacts at random to balance the scales?"

"I don't pretend to have the answers," Bolan said. "And even if I did, we couldn't settle it tonight. Maybe Luis can find you someplace safe and dry to sleep. Whatever happens, I expect a busy day tomorrow."

"Busy fighting? Killing?"

"I suppose we could surrender, if the rebels come around. That way, nobody dies but us."

"I've never known a soldier who was so glib," Travis said.

"Known many?"

Something in her attitude relaxed a little. "You're the first," she admitted.

"Well, I'm sorry that you couldn't start with someone more agreeable. A nice recruiting sergeant, maybe. Promise you the world and give you KP twice a week."

"KP?"

"Forget it." Bolan shifted gears. "If they show up tomorrow—"

"The guerrillas?"

"Right. If they show up, you can't expect to do much with a butcher knife. Try to get out of here. I doubt they'll have enough men to surround the place. Not thoroughly. Just try to get away."

"And then what?" Travis asked.

"Survive," he said. "Carry the tale."

"Go tell the Spartans?" Travis blushed. "Sorry. I wasn't mocking you. I only meant—"

"I know the story," Bolan said. "In this case, though, we are the Spartans. If it goes the same for us, somebody needs to spread the word."

"I'll try," she promised, and he heard a small catch in her voice.

"And once you're moving," he suggested, "don't look back."

22

Against all odds, there was no trouble from the hostages. Anticipating that at least a few of them would try to slip away while he was sleeping, Paco Alvarez sat up all night to watch his sentries watching them. It proved to be a fruitless exercise and left him weary when the time came to resume their march, but Alvarez felt better for it all the same. If something else went wrong, no matter who was blamed for it, at least he'd know that it was not his fault.

The runners he had ordered to retrieve all village stragglers had come back within the time limit and brought five extra prisoners. Although he knew there might be more still hiding in the forest, Alvarez was not prepared to spend any time in fruitless searching, so he settled for the thirty-five and drove them on until it was time to make camp for the night.

Alvarez was pleased that he'd accomplished his mission without a single killing, though he was prepared to make examples of his prisoners along he way, if any gave him trouble. Thirty-five was more than he'd expected to deliver, even granting that a few of them were elderly or children, scarcely fit to work. Cruz might not like the prisoners he brought, but Alvarez had carried out his orders to the letter.

And when the time came to eliminate all witnesses, he'd do the same again.

He was supposed to meet Cruz and Aguirre, with their

party, near the junction of two sluggish jungle rivers, where the waters merged to flow southward as one. His landmark was a rocky crag that poked above the forest canopy, where eagles nested and the forest cleared enough to let them hunt. So far, he was on schedule for a rendezvous at midday.

Almost as if responding to his thought, one of his men suddenly called out for help from midway down the marching column's length. Shouting an order for the rest to halt and watch their captives closely, Alvarez jogged back to find one of his men holding two villagers at gunpoint while a third lay sprawled beside him on the ground, face smeared with blood.

"What happened?" Alvarez demanded.

His man jerked his rifle's muzzle toward the figure on the ground. "He tried to run. These two were just about to follow him."

Alvarez stood before them, weighing options. He could execute the fallen villager, cut down the two accomplices to make a point, but he was worried that a shooting might spark a revolt among the hostages. They were unarmed and bound to lose, but he had come this far with all of them intact and only had a few more hours left before the burden of their sullen hatred would be shared with other guards.

Decision made, he spoke to the two uninjured hostages. "You are his friends?" he asked them, nodding toward the still-unconscious third.

Reluctantly, they nodded silent affirmation.

"Good," Alvarez said. "In that case you'll be glad to carry him until he's fit to walk. And if for any reason he's unable to perform his work at journey's end, you'll gladly do it for him."

The men exchanged hasty glances and bobbed their heads.

"I can't hear you," Alvarez complained.

"Yes," one of them replied.

"Yes, what?" he pressed, angling his weapon toward the foot of space between them, ready to stitch one or both if they defied him.

"Yes, sir," both voices chorused, almost synchronized.

"Perfect," Alvarez said. "We've wasted time enough already."

To the sentry standing by, he added, "You did well. The next time any of them breaks formation, kill all three."

"Yes, Captain!"

Alvarez smiled, wishing a field promotion was that easy to obtain, but he did not correct the soldier. Ego boosts were always welcome when they came with no annoying strings attached. The soldier was clearly relieved that Alvarez had not been critical, and so his gratitude spilled over into flattery. Or maybe he was simply ignorant of ranks within the movement. Either way, the momentary lapse in protocol did no one any harm.

Resuming his position near the column's head, he passed the word to march again and hold a steady pace. They had approximately five miles left to go before they reached the point where he had to wait for Cruz and company, unless the main force reached the rendezvous ahead of them. In either case, he hoped to make no further stops along the way.

So far, so good, Alvarez thought. He had asserted his authority over the hostages without unnecessary violence, while demonstrating that his kindness should not be confused with weakness.

If another of them tested him, he would have blood.

Cruz would expect no less, and Alvarez did not intend to disappoint his friend, the father of their cause. The slaves would be delivered come what may, at any cost, and damn who ever tried to stop him from completing his assignment.

Smiling to himself, he marched on.

IT WAS IMPOSSIBLE to say with any certainty from which direction danger might approach Site X. Compelled to use his own best judgment, Bolan noted that the rebels led by Paco Alvarez should come from the southwest, assuming that the ruined city was their destination in the first place.

On the other hand, they could be going somewhere else en-

tirely, leaving Bolan and his small squad of defenders on edge
without any enemy to face.

In either case, the Executioner had done his best to be
prepared.

He'd made a sat phone call to Hal Brognola in the States,
providing the coordinates for Site X via GPS. Whatever happened in the next few hours or days, the big Fed could pull
any diplomatic strings he thought appropriate to safeguard or
eliminate the ancient treasure trove. That problem was removed from Bolan's hands, and since he couldn't blitz the city
even if he'd wanted to, he turned his thoughts and energy to
its defense.

That was another king-size order, given the supplies and
personnel on hand. In terms of killing from a distance, Bolan's
team had two rifles, two shotguns, his Beretta and six frag grenades, three bows and one blowgun. Selecting fields of fire
was problematic, but he compensated for the scarcity of troops
by placing C-4 charges where he thought they might be useful, each implanted with a detonator keyed to Bolan's radio-
remote trigger device. If things got hairy, he could blow the
charges all at once or pick and choose like Claymore mines,
positioned to defend his long perimeter.

It wasn't much, but he could only work with what he had.
The villagers who'd joined him, seasoned hunters all, listened to Bolan's thoughts, translated by Luis Candera, and
suggested some adjustments he'd found acceptable. He left
the bow hunters and blowgun artist to decide where they
could best defend the city and themselves, without obstructing others' fields of fire. The fifty-something ax man was assigned to stay with Carrie Travis while she prowled around
the ruins, and to help her hide—or better yet, to slip away—
if Alvarez and his guerrillas made the scene.

It wasn't a defensive line that Bolan would've chosen, if
he'd had a choice, but circumstances always altered cases. He
had faith that his companions would resist invasion to the best

of their ability, and little doubt that some of them would die in the attempt.

For Bolan's part, he had the Steyr AUG and a dozen magazines, for five hundred rounds in 5.56 mm. The Beretta and its five magazines gave him another seventy-six 9 mm Parabellum rounds. In theory, if he made every shot count, he could drop almost six hundred men himself before he started pitching hand grenades.

But the Executioner knew that combat never was that tidy. Some of his shots were bound to miss, more of them if he fired in full-auto or 3-round-burst mode to sweep the line and put his human targets down emphatically. Nobody shot a perfect score in battle, when the air was full of smoke, shrapnel and screams. If every bullet found its mark, no one would ever leave a battleground alive.

From his vantage point atop a vine-encrusted building, reached by outer stairs grown thick with grass and lichen, Bolan scanned Site X until he caught a glimpse of Travis and her escort emerging from the same doorway where she had paused with Bolan at dusk the previous day. He had loaned her a flashlight, assuming that she would run down the batteries in nothing flat. He held his one set of replacements in reserve.

The preliminary search was bound to frustrate her, Bolan thought, since she had no proper equipment, not even a camera. Parts of the site had been despoiled, while others were pristine. Or, as close to it as any place could be after a thousand years or more of nonstop exposure to tropical weather, flora and fauna. Where tombs and other buildings were untouched by looters, Travis had no means of gaining access other than her borrowed knife and her companion's double-bladed ax. Bolan had read the disappointment on her face, something akin to grief, when she informed him that she wouldn't breach the other buildings without proper tools and personnel, observing all the standard scientific protocols.

He recognized that kind of dedication and appreciated it. He also left her to it, rather than observing that she might not have another chance to delve within the city's secrets if she didn't get it done that morning, with the meager tools at hand. Why dwell upon the fact that they could all be dead before nightfall, if Travis hadn't grasped it yet?

Site X had managed to conceal the bones of its first kings for a millennium or more. As he sat and waited for his enemies to show themselves, Bolan could only wonder whether it would be his final resting place, as well.

If so, at least he would have company.

The Executioner would not go down alone.

He felt regret that Carrie Travis and the others might die with him, but the choice was ultimately theirs. Bolan supposed he could've had worse company to die in, but he wasn't ready to concede defeat.

Not yet.

Whoever came to take the treasure from them would discover that a hefty price remained. And they would have to pay that tab in blood.

"THEY ARE COMING, Commander!"

Alejandro Cruz rose from his place on the boulder where he had been seated for the past half hour, smooth stone pressing hard against his buttocks until they were almost numb. Tomas Aguirre stood beside him, anxious looking, as Cruz waited for the last detachment of his men to show themselves.

He had arrived on point ahead of schedule, having pushed his troops for extra speed, then felt a simmering, irrational annoyance that the others, led by Paco Alvarez were not there waiting for him. He'd kept it to himself, but Cruz could not help brooding over the suspicion that they'd somehow sacrificed a critical advantage.

"Right on time," Aguirre said, after consulting his wristwatch. His cheerful demeanor turned up the heat on Cruz's irritation, but the rebel leader kept his face deadpan. It wouldn't do to chastise his subordinates for following his orders to the letter and the minute. On the other hand, if Alvarez had failed to bring the laborers they needed…

"There he is," Aguirre declared needlessly, as Alvarez came into view. "And look! I'd say he's brought us thirty, maybe forty extra hands."

Cruz went to greet his chief lieutenant, first returning Alvarez's crisp salute, then shaking hands. He asked, "How many have you brought to help us?"

"Thirty-five," Alvarez responded. "All the village had. But some of them are children or old."

With a slight frown, Cruz replied, "I see them. Well, if this is all that you could find, so be it."

Alvarez hid his disappointment well. It took a friend of many years to see that he was stung by Cruz's words.

"I'll supervise them personally," Alvarez declared. "Each one will work until he drops."

"With our own men, it may just be enough," Cruz said.

"Oh, we can do the job with these," Aguirre interrupted. "As for how long it will take, that's anybody's guess. I'm not sure either of you understands how much there is to shift."

"I want it all," Cruz said. "Whatever can be sold, or melted down if need be."

"Then with this lot," Aguirre said, "and with no vehicles and leaving out the men you'll need to guard the others, I'd expect it to take two weeks, minimum."

"So be it. Do what must be done."

"The first job is to get there," Aguirre said. "Are we leaving soon?"

"At once," Cruz replied. He turned to Alvarez. "That is, if you are ready to proceed?"

"At your command, sir."

Cruz nodded, nearly satisfied, and shouted at his troops, "Up and away! Follow the scouts and hold formation. Watch the prisoners as if your very lives depended on it, since they do."

He scanned the faces turned in his direction, hoping that he might find one with an expression he could fasten on, someone he could lash for insubordination, but they offered no hint of resistance. Even the prisoners seemed wearily resigned to what awaited them, as if their fate had been determined by the gods.

And who could say that it had not?

They marched, his scouts setting pace to match the urgency of Cruz's orders as they left the clearing near the point where rivers merged and struck off to the north, with flowing water on their right most of the way.

Cruz stayed inside his own mind for the most part, conscious of the steps he took, the obstacles that nature placed in front of him, but still preoccupied with what had to be accomplished once they reached the city. If they had it to themselves, work could begin at once, without delay. His men and their new labor force would work from dawn to dusk, as many days as were required to see the job completed and the extra witnesses eliminated.

But if others held the place against them, they would first be forced to fight.

Cruz was prepared for that, as well. He had brought every soldier readily available to him within the time allowed—although it came to less than half of the GPLF's total membership. The rest were scattered far and wide from Flores to the streets of Guatemala City, with rural troops encamped at several far-flung hideaways. Cruz wished there had been time to rally all of them and bring three hundred men to strip the Mayan city of its riches, but his haste had not permitted any action of the sort.

He was troubled by a sudden thought. What would his soldiers do if he was taken from them suddenly, upon an ancient killing ground? Would they fight on, or quit the movement in dismay? If Paco Alvarez did not survive him, who would lead the Guatemalan People's Liberation Front to final victory?

And it occurred to Cruz that it need not concern him. He could only lead the struggle while he lived, and having once renounced all faith in a hereafter, he could not presume to think that he would watch his former soldiers from on high, as they fought on to victory or death.

He had abandoned superstition for that very reason, so that it could not command his life. What happened next was his choice. Cruz knew he had to weigh the circumstances, watch himself, choose wisely in all things—or suffer the inevitable consequences.

He would have the Mayan treasure, Cruz decided.

It was victory or death.

23

"There's just so much to do, and I don't have the proper—"

Carrie Travis caught herself and left the comment dangling, forever unfinished. She smiled apologetically at her escort, whose knowledge of English seemingly extended only to a few choice epithets. Her bronze-skinned bodyguard returned a gap-toothed smile.

She didn't mind having an escort in the ruins. Travis realized her own shortcomings, knew she couldn't tell deadly snakes from harmless ones or spot the insects that could kill her where she stood. And she agreed with Cooper's judgment that Luis Candera was the only fit interpreter for Cooper's orders to the other men. Still, Travis wished her escort was able to address her with some phrase besides the ever-ready "son-of-bitch bastard."

Or worse.

His name was Julio, and Travis didn't want to know where he had learned his terse English vocabulary. Likewise, even if they had been able to communicate, she probably would not have asked about his ax. He kept it clean and sharp, but there were dark stains on the wooden handle, just below the double-bladed head, that brought a frown unbidden to her face.

Not that an ax would help them if guerrillas turned up on the scene with automatic weapons and who knew what else. Paul Bunyan would be no use to them then. Matt Cooper would be useful, she supposed—although she hadn't seen him fight—and Travis reckoned that Candera's men would hold their own, with a home court advantage. But she didn't need a diploma from West Point to know they'd be outnumbered and outgunned.

In other words, they were likely to be killed.

That prospect terrified her. She had been able to suppress her fears so far—throughout the funeral arrangements for her father, the decision to pursue his work in Guatemala, and the hardships that had dogged her in the jungle. She'd been scared when the guerrillas had captured her, of course, but even then it hadn't been like this.

Why now? she asked herself.

Perhaps, she thought, because redemption was within her grasp, and now the enemy proposed to snatch it all away. The evidence to vindicate her father's reputation lay beneath her feet and all around her, proof no ivory tower snobs could possibly deny. And it would make her reputation, too, establish Carrie Travis as a first-rank archaeologist worthy of mention in textbooks and lectures. This dig alone could keep her busy for the rest of her career, professionally set for life.

But life as Carrie Travis knew it could be ending any minute. The enemy could drop in for a chat five minutes or five days from now, and when the shooting started she would be out of luck.

Cooper had advised her to evacuate at the first sign of trouble. Barely armed, without supplies of any kind and hopeless when it came to blazing trails, Travis had doubts that she would last one night alone, much less make her way back to Flores and what passed for civilization on the Guatemalan frontier.

Better to stay and face the enemy, perhaps. Let the inevitable happen quickly, without making it a trial by ordeal. Still, what could she do with a pathetic borrowed knife? She had used butcher knives before, but only on the cuts of meat her grocer sold, never in a situation where the meat was armed and dangerous.

And still…Site X!

Her mind reeled with the treasures she had seen so far, just in the buildings violated by guerrilla looting parties. There was so much that they hadn't taken yet, and she could only guess what waited to be found in the structures they hadn't breached.

You'll never know, the devil on her shoulder jeered.

And maybe he was right. She didn't have the gear to properly explore the looted tombs, much less to open new ones and record their contents for posterity. For science. Anything she tried to do on this trip would be bumbling, amateurish, ruining the site for those who followed after her. Someone would have the honor of exploring Site X and revealing all its mysteries, but Travis didn't think she'd be in a position to participate.

Cooper was planning for a battle, had his meager band of soldiers staked out in the ruins with their ancient firearms, bows, whatever. It reminded Travis of the Alamo, except she had no reason to believe they would survive for thirteen days.

· Try thirteen minutes, she thought, if the GPLF hit them with a serious assault, guns blazing, lobbing hand grenades, whatever soldiers did at times like that. Cooper was just one man, his backup barely there.

If she was leaving, Travis thought she should be on her way *before* the trouble started. Take her chances in the jungle without waiting for the enemy to move in and surround them. But she couldn't bring herself to run. Not yet. It would've felt like spitting on her father's memory, his dreams.

"Looks like I'm screwed," she told her sidekick. "What about you?"

He grinned again and answered, "Son-of-bitch bastard."

"I hear you, brother," Travis said. She laughed.

"ALL SET FOR DOOMSDAY?" Travis asked.

Turning to face her, Bolan nodded. "We're as ready as we'll ever be, with what we've got."

"That call you made," she said. "Should we expect the cavalry?"

"It's possible," Bolan said, "but I wouldn't count on it."

"Okay. So this is it, then." Travis seemed resigned, but not especially depressed. "I've always hoped it would be quick, instead of lingering. You know, step off the curb and there's the taxicab you didn't hail. Lights out."

"We're not dead yet," Bolan reminded her.

"But if these GPLF guys show up, the odds are on their side."

"Odds tell you probability. They don't predict the future," Bolan said.

"I take it you've come through some other situations similar to this?" There was a trace of hope in the woman's voice, her attitude.

"Minus the pyramids," Bolan replied. "I've bucked the odds a time or two."

"So tell me," she pressed on. "Why don't we just get out of here right now? Is there a point in fighting when we're almost sure to lose?"

"The point, for me," he said, "is that I have a job to do. As for yourself, I'll say again that I encourage you to go."

"Just leave you here," she said.

"How can you help me if you stay?" he asked.

"I'm working on it. Anyway, out there—" she waved a hand expansively toward the surrounding rain forest "—I'm toast."

"We've talked about this," he reminded her. "Your chances in the bush are better than your odds of living through a firefight here."

"With my luck," she said, with a half-smile, "that cavalry would show up just about the time I'm out of earshot. You'd go winging back to Fort Machismo, or wherever you came from, while I'd just walk around in circles until some jaguar needs a snack."

"Take someone with you," he suggested.

"What, and steal a quarter of your army?" Travis shook her head. "I'm thinking you need every man you've got."

She wasn't wrong. Noting her evident determination, Bolan changed the subject. "What about your exploration? How's it going?"

"Not much I can really do without the proper hardware and support," Travis replied. "But just between us hopeless cases, it's the greatest thing I've ever seen. This place will make careers, if it survives. Hell, I could work here for the rest of my professional life." She paused, frowning, and said, "I don't suppose you've got an inkling as to how long that might be?"

"They could show up at any time," Bolan explained, "or not for days."

"In which case, we'll be starving, as well as surrounded."

"We've got some fair hunters among us," he told her.

"No doubt. But can you spare them for a jaunt into the woods? I mean, we're sitting here on red alert, unless I missed the bulletin that it was all a big mistake. Who leaves his post, a time like that?"

"I've got two of them in the forest now," Bolan said.

Travis blinked at him, surprised. "Hunting?"

"For people."

"Ah. The old search-and-destroy routine."

"Search and report," Bolan corrected. "Any warning we can get will help us."

"Gives you time to spring the trap, instead of having their trap sprung on you," she said.

"Something like that."

Soberly she asked, "How many will you kill?"

"If it comes down to that," Bolan replied, "as many as I can."

"It doesn't bother you?"

"I'll take it over the alternative," he said.

"I'm serious."

"Me, too," Bolan said. "Combat is a killing business. It's

what soldiers train and study for. To stay alive and make sure that your adversary doesn't."

"And somebody's got to do it, right?"

"Sometimes," Bolan agreed, ignoring her sarcasm. "That's exactly right. Some people—certain predators—aren't into civilized debate. They want it all, they want it now, and they're prepared to take it over your dead body. Some prefer it that way, killing even if they have a chance to steal without bloodletting. Force is all they understand, and death's the only thing that slows them."

"I want to help you," Travis said, surprising him. "I mean, if you can think of anything for me to do that won't make matters worse. I realize I'm damn near useless, but—"

"We'll think of something," Bolan promised her.

"Okay. I guess you don't need anyone to load the muskets or boil water for the wounded. How about—"

Her thought was interrupted by a whistle from the nearby pyramid. Turning to face the sound, Bolan observed Luis Candera pointing toward the dark southeastern tree line, where a running figure had appeared.

One of the scouts.

The runner called ahead in Spanish, rattling it off so quickly that Bolan was unable to translate.

But Candera did it for him. "They are coming," he called out. "Forty or fifty men, and all the people from my village."

24

His last two hours on the trail were the worst torture that Alejandro Cruz had ever felt. It was not physical discomfort that tormented him. He had survived police interrogation. He had marched on hotter days through worse terrain. Rather, it was the uncertainty within himself, the grim sense of foreboding that he could not shake.

Over the past few miles, Cruz had become obsessed with the idea that he would reach the ancient city and discover soldiers camped there by the hundreds, the whole site a frenzied beehive of activity. Or worse, that he would find it looted and abandoned, worthless to him, with no clue to tell him where the precious artifacts had gone.

When it began to rain again, for the third time that morning, Cruz muttered a curse against the sky and nature. They conspired against him, turning solid earth to mud beneath his feet, retarding progress as his party slogged on toward the treasure of a lifetime.

The Mayan treasure was like a blessing from the Heaven he did not believe in. Now that it was on the verge of being snatched away—might already be gone—he felt as though he'd plunged into the depths of Hell.

It was ridiculous, perhaps a symptom of insanity, but Cruz could not deny his feelings. He could only hide them from the others, most particularly from Alvarez. There could be no aspersions cast upon his loyalty to the struggle. Otherwise, his men might turn upon him and demand their pound of flesh for having been deceived.

The last mile nearly broke him, rain and sweat drenching his limp fatigues, mud clotted on his feet until Cruz felt as if his boots were blocks of lead. He nearly dropped his rifle once, glancing around to see if anyone had noticed, and he caught one of the hostage children staring at him with a mournful look that seemed to offer pity in the place of fear.

At last, when Cruz was certain he could stand no more, fearing he'd lost the strength to take another step, one of the scouts returned and told him that they'd reached the city. Cruz lurched forward, fought his way over the final fifty yards, and stopped short where the ruins loomed beneath a slate-gray sky. He slumped against a tree, heedless of ants or any other insects lurking there, and scanned the ruins, trembling as he sought the evidence to verify his gloomy visions.

Certainly, Cruz saw no soldiers, trucks or helicopters. There were no cranes lifting giant blocks of stone, no gangs of workmen sweating over picks and shovels. Sniffing at the sodden breeze, Cruz smelled no residue of dynamite or other high explosives.

That disposed of one nightmare, but Cruz still feared that they had come too late. He would press on and find the treasure vaults despoiled, yawning and empty. He could *feel* it, like a fist clutching his gut.

Cruz fought the urge to rush ahead and find out for himself, charge through the ruins on his own and check each edifice in turn. He had survived too long in war to take that risk, even in his present distracted state.

Turning, Cruz beckoned half a dozen of his men to join him at the tree line. Two of them had seen the Mayan city previously, while the other four stood gaping, suitably impressed. He issued orders in a whisper, worried that his voice might carry to the ruins and alert whatever adversaries might be hidden there.

"Fan out and check the ruins," Cruz instructed. "Watch for traps and any evidence of recent digging. When you're finished, come back and report."

Heads bobbed around the semicircle with a muttering of "Yes, sir" from each in turn. Cruz stepped aside and let them pass, tracking their progress from his shadowed hiding place.

No gunshots echoed from the ruined city as his men entered the weed-choked ancient streets and moved among the buildings. One by one they disappeared from view. Cruz glimpsed them here and there, occasionally, as their search proceeded, but they all resembled one another from a distance. Chafing at the time it took to carry out his order, Cruz was on the verge of sending in a backup team when one of his advance men suddenly appeared and started walking back.

The soldier moved with sluggish, almost wooden steps, arms hanging at his sides. It took another beat for Cruz to realize that the young man was empty-handed. He had left his rifle somewhere in the ruins.

What was he thinking, to go wandering unarmed around a place like this, when—

Suddenly the soldier toppled forward, dropping facedown into the earth without raising a hand to break his fall. Cruz gasped involuntarily as he beheld a feathered shaft protruding from the downed man's back, between his shoulder blades.

Cruz barked more orders at his soldiers, sending half his troop of fifty—forty-four, if the other five point men were dead as well—to rush the ruined city, find the Indians who challenged him and root them out.

It might be Paco's fault, he thought. If he had missed someone when he was cleaning out the native village, then—

The first explosion rocked Cruz on his heels and sent two of his soldiers catapulting skyward, tumbling through a cloud of smoke and dust before they fell back to the ground.

IT WAS A TOSS-UP with the first half-dozen rebels sent to scour the city. Bolan could've let them pass unharmed, to draw the others in, but there was still a chance they'd notice something, maybe spot one of the villagers or even mount the steps to Bolan's sniper nest. Instead, he'd raised a fist above his head and pumped it once, then let Candera's people do what they did best.

It was a fluke that one guerrilla made it halfway back to where his friends were hiding in the forest. Something in his physiology, perhaps, let him cover those last yards of ground before he fell, despite the arrow buried within millimeters of his spine.

What happened next had been another fifty-fifty shot. One option was a headlong charge, the other swift encirclement to trap the enemy within. Bolan supposed his adversaries would suspect a native hunting party taken by surprise, anticipating easy victory when M-16s were matched against the hunting tools of Guatemalan primitives.

But they were in for a surprise.

The Executioner was ready when a skirmish line of riflemen erupted from the trees, racing across the nearly open ground southeast of where he waited. While he didn't have the time to count precisely, Bolan estimated there were some two dozen shooters in the party. All had automatic weapons at the ready, running with their shoulders hunched and faces set in grim expressions. Killing faces, ready to avenge the execution of their friends.

He beat them to it, ticking off the yardage in his head and watching as they neared the scrap of fabric he had posted as his first range marker. It was tied on the reverse side of a fallen log, invisible to watchers in the forest but as clear as day to Bolan, even in the shadows of a murky afternoon.

He waited with the radio-remote trigger device in hand, one charge selected from among the dozen he had planted. As the skirmish line approached their point of no return, his thumb pressed lightly on the detonator's button, mashing harder on it as a pair of rebels vaulted across the rotting log.

The C-4 charge erupted beneath them like the first belch of a small volcano, instantly enveloping both men in dust and smoke. They flew forward like a pair of acrobatic clowns, arms flailing, bodies twisting in defiance of their normal structure, crashing down to earth a few short yards apart.

Whether the two were dead or merely injured, Bolan didn't know. He was preoccupied with their companions at the moment, leveling his Steyr AUG and peering through its sight to find another mark.

The nearest runners to the fallen pair were dazed and reeling, firing aimlessly into the ruins as if noise alone could save them. Farther off to either side, the rest kept coming, many of them also firing, their bullets snipping ferns and creepers, whining as they ricocheted from ancient stone.

Bolan lined up a shot and took it, drilled his man with one round through the chest and left him thrashing out the final seconds of his life amid the rotten vegetation of the forest floor. Before his tumbling brass touched down beside him, Bolan heard the Springfield's first shot echo through the ruins, louder than the stutter of the M-16s, followed immediately by the throaty *boom* of shotguns. He could not pick out the whisper of an arrow's passage through the maelstrom, but he saw one strike a sprinting rebel, pierce his shoulder in-and-out to take him down.

Battle was joined, and Bolan had no time to think of Carrie Travis, of the treasure, or of anything beyond surviving to his next shot, and the next one after that.

THE SHOCK of the explosion, followed by gunfire rattling through the ancient ruins, drove a spike of pain between the narrowed eyes of Paco Alvarez. He hadn't glimpsed the enemy, but knew that he would be sent to root them out.

"Paco!" The voice of Alejandro Cruz was so tight that it fairly cracked from strain.

"Yes, sir," Alvarez replied, moving to stand beside his friend and commander.

"Leave me half a dozen men to guard the prisoners," Cruz ordered. "Take the rest and sweep the city. Find these bastards and exterminate them! I want no one left alive to challenge us!"

"Yes, sir!"

He spared a quick glance for Aguirre, standing just behind Cruz with a sick expression on his face, as if he couldn't believe what was happening. Alvarez experienced a brief desire to kill Aguirre where he stood, punish the mercenary for discovering the ruins and their treasure in the first place, bringing this hell down upon his shoulders. But the moment passed.

Alvarez moved among the soldiers, picking out the six youngest to stay behind. The others seemed eager to join the action, mix it up in battle and avenge themselves against the strangers who had killed their comrades. Their clenched teeth, narrowed eyes, white-knuckled grips around their weapons told him they were ready.

"Follow me!" he ordered, turning toward the ruins in full faith that they would do as they were told. No fool himself, Alvarez led them for the first few yards, then slowed his pace enough for half of them to pass him, charging on into the city in the middle of the pack.

It was a piece of simple logic, really. Alvarez was no good to them if a bullet found him in his first few seconds on the battlefield. He could not rally, guide or save them if his voice was stilled in death. It was a leader's duty to survive, if only for his men.

Another blast rattled the world, followed by screams away to Alvarez's left. It couldn't be artillery, because he heard no echo of a shot before the detonation, yet the blasts were far too powerful for hand grenades.

A mortar?

It was possible, but seemed unlikely. Even with so many weapons firing, Alvarez should still have heard the sound a mortar made as it discharged a shell. And where on Earth would native bow hunters acquire a mortar?

Through the first rush of adrenaline, he realized that M-16s were not the only weapons firing on the field. At least one rifle of some larger caliber was laying down sporadic fire, accompanied by one or two shotguns. And there were arrows too, like the slim shaft that had erupted from the chest of a guerrilla to his right, causing the man to slump and fall. The arrow held the man's full weight for a moment, with its feathered end planted in soil, then gravity took over the soldier's squirming body sucked the shaft inside itself, one slow inch at a time.

Alvarez didn't stay to watch the show. He ran on toward the nearest structure draped in creepers, watching shadows up ahead, holding his fire. There were too many of his own men in the way for random shooting. He would find a target, mark it, and be certain of it when he made his kill.

The enemy was almost close enough to taste.

CARRIE TRAVIS FELT as if the world were ending and she was trapped at the chaotic epicenter of its destruction. Her ears rang and her mind reeled from explosions, gunfire, angry shouts and cries from the wounded or dying.

She huddled in the doorway of a looted tomb with cobwebs tangled in her hair. Julio crouched beside her, clinging to his ax and following the action with a bland expression. Travis couldn't tell if he was frightened or excited by the fighting, if he wanted to wade in or wished that he could run away.

Travis had fought the urge to flee since they were warned of enemies approaching. It took all her strength of will to keep from running now, and she recalled her promise to Matt Cooper that she *would* run, get away by any means and take their story somewhere, anywhere. But when the shooting started she felt paralyzed, and by the time she had regained control the battle had surrounded her. She no longer had anywhere to go.

At some point, she realized, she had to have drawn her borrowed knife. It was a feather in her hand, useless against the guns, but she felt marginally better just for holding it. Whether she'd have the guts to use it was another question. Travis still had hopes that she might not be forced to fight, but they were fading rapidly.

A sound of running footsteps made her shrink into shadows, fairly cringing, while her escort kept his place. A moment later, two men she had never seen stopped in the doorway, crouching slightly as they peered into the darkness. Travis hoped they might move on in search of targets, but that hope was dashed when her companion sprang at them and struck the taller of them with his ax, splitting the shooter's skull.

The dead man slumped, and before Julio had an opportunity to wrench his ax free the other rebel fired a point-blank burst into his chest. It had to have been off center, from the way it spun him on his heels, and Travis didn't know she had cried out until her own voice echoed back at her from someplace deeper in the tomb.

The lone guerrilla froze, straining his eyes again to penetrate the darkness of her hiding place. Perhaps he'd recognized a woman's voice, for he did not immediately fire another burst into the shadows. Rather, edging closer, he approached Travis without observing her, moving like a blind man.

Travis held her breath, afraid that he would hear if she exhaled. In nothing flat her lungs were aching, burning, straining to betray her with a gasp for air. As the intruder moved within arm's reach, small flecks of light swam in her vision, nature's light show urging her to breathe or else release her grip on consciousness.

With an explosive gasp, she lunged, driving the butcher knife beneath her enemy's right arm. As he recoiled from the assault, her free hand clutched his ammo belt and held him fast. She felt her blade's tip grate along a rib, then sink into the space between it and its neighbor.

Gunfire and a howl of pain reverberated through the Mayan tomb. Wild ricochets struck sparks from stony walls, whining like noisemakers on Independence Day. The assailant stumbled, fell, and Travis fell on top of him, her weight sinking the foot-long blade as deep as it could go. The man jerked underneath her in a ghastly parody of sex, while Travis used her free hand to divert his weapon's muzzle, praying that he'd die or else run out of ammunition before a ricochet burned through her flesh.

She got her wish.

The gunman shuddered one last time, gasped something in a dialect she didn't understand, and then went limp. Only when she rose was Travis aware of his blood soaking though her shirt and pants, painting her hands and arms.

She left the knife protruding from his abdomen, reached for his rifle, then decided that it might be empty. There was a process for reloading, but she didn't know it, so she passed him by and risked a step outside the tomb to claim the other rebel's weapon.

Was it loaded? Was the safety on or off? She didn't know, but reckoned that she'd learn the answers to her questions soon enough.

She had a choice to make.

Trembling, she went to find Matt Cooper in the midst of death.

25

Bolan found his mark, took up the trigger slack, then eased off as his target stiffened, reached up toward the blowgun dart protruding from his neck, then toppled over on his back. From the convulsions that ensued, Bolan determined that the dart had packed a little something extra on its tip.

A bullet spanged off stone immediately to his left, and Bolan spun in that direction, dropping to a crouch. He wasn't sure where it had come from, somewhere down below and to the west. His little squad was more or less surrounded, and he wondered briefly whether Carrie Travis had been able to get out.

Or if she'd even tried.

There was no time to worry about that. Another bullet whispered overhead, and this time Bolan thought he had the sniper marked. One of them, anyway. Rising from where he'd sheltered on the far side of a fallen tree, the rifleman sprinted to reach the recessed doorway of a nearby building, screened with vines.

Bad choice.

Bolan retrieved his detonator, keyed the proper charge and thumbed the button for ignition. Sixty yards away, the recess where his adversary hid erupted with a thunderclap. Its arch collapsed, a roiling dust cloud blocking Bolan's view of his opponent.

Fair enough. He'd count that as a kill unless the rebel rose again to challenge him. If he was breathing, it would take an excavation team to get him out of there, and all his friends were busy at the moment.

Bolan scanned the battlefield again, in search of Paco Alvarez or Alejandro Cruz, but they were nowhere to be seen. He'd caught a glimpse of Alvarez during the second rush, but missed his chance to drop the GPLF's second in command when a near-miss had sent him reeling backward from the temple's parapet. Now he would have to take what he could get and hope that his companions were in shape to do the same.

He still heard firing from the Springfield, but its source had shifted from the early moments of the battle. Only one shotgun was still in action, but he couldn't tell if enemies had snuffed the other shooter, or if he'd simply run out of ammunition. As for Bolan's volunteers who carried silent weapons, he could only track their progress when an arrow or a dart struck home in front of him and brought another rebel down.

So far, Bolan thought, they were holding their own. With fifty or sixty guerrillas against them, they'd already killed or wounded roughly one in five, a respectable showing by any standards.

But it wasn't enough.

They could kill half of their enemies, even two-thirds, and still lose the fight if enough adversaries remained to root them out and finish them. One man could do it, if he had the nerve, the skill, the luck. Bolan himself had beaten more intimidating odds and lived to fight again.

But this time he was on defense, a static game that often limited mobility and thereby tipped advantage to the other side.

It would be touch and go, he realized, until the last guerrilla had been killed or forced into retreat.

And that was why he had to move.

Lying in wait for hours or for days to make the perfect shot was something Bolan had endured as a sniper, in another life, but it was not a skill that served him well when he was being overrun.

He had to meet the enemy below and take the war to them, or he could kiss it all goodbye. Whatever magic Brognola was trying to perform in Washington, it wouldn't help him at the moment.

Bolan backtracked to the stairs that served his roost, checked them for enemies and found himself alone. Seizing the opportunity, he took the ancient stairs three at a time, rushing to join the fight.

TOMAS AGUIRRE CLUTCHED his borrowed M-16 and huddled in the shadow of a structure that he hadn't breached during his other visits to the Mayan city. He had no idea what lay inside, if anything, and at the moment heaps of gold would not have tempted him.

Aguirre didn't want to die, and he was terrified that he was running out of time.

The treasure hunter's life was often hazardous. He'd faced his share of danger in the wilds of Mexico, Honduras, Panama and Guatemala, but this was his first pitched battle and he wanted out. Cruz wasn't paying him enough to sacrifice his life this way—but now that battle had been joined, Aguirre couldn't find an exit.

Move! Do something!

The advice was sound, but translating his thoughts to action was more difficult. Each time Aguirre poked his head out of the niche he'd found, a bullet or an arrow whispered past and nearly struck his face. He didn't think that Cruz's men would kill him for the fun of it, but they were running wild, and the enemies he hadn't glimpsed were throwing everything they had into the fight.

It had been foolish, thinking he could slip into the city on his own and grab a bit of treasure for himself while Cruz and his guerrillas were distracted. If he'd had a time machine, Aguirre would have spun the dial and changed the past ten minutes, used that precious time to get away from Cruz and leave the rebels on their own to pacify the enemy. But his greed had got the best of him.

Again.

This time, it seemed as if it might prove fatal.

Forget about the gold, Aguirre told himself. Get out and hide until they're finished, then come back and take a bow for fighting like a hero.

Who would ever know the difference?

Aguirre crept from cover, moving in a crouch that made his back and thigh muscles protest. He stubbornly ignored the pain, preferring it to bullet wounds or dropping with an arrow through his lungs.

Who fought with *arrows* in this day and age? he wondered.

Aguirre was surprised to find that he had crossed a hundred yards of somewhat open ground between the tree line and his latest hiding place. He wouldn't have to run that far, however, to conceal himself from danger in the trees. No more than fifty yards from where he stood, the jungle waited for him, growing darker by the moment as the sun slid westward and prepared to vanish for the night.

He moved in that direction, flicking cautious glances left and right to watch his flanks. Aguirre's first glimpse of the woman startled him, made him suspect he was hallucinating. But he looked again and saw her clearly, striding through the ruins with a rifle in her hands.

He raised his weapon, sighted on her, certain there were no female guerrillas in the Guatemalan People's Liberation Front. For all its high-flown rhetoric, the movement harbored too much archaic machismo for a female soldier to be welcomed in its ranks.

That made the woman one of Cruz's enemies, and by extension, one of those who'd tried to kill Aguirre. He could drop her where she stood, a relatively easy shot—or he could take her prisoner.

It struck Aguirre that a woman warrior might be even more

unusual among the local natives than within the rebel movement. He could only guess what she might represent to those now fighting in the ruins to defend their ancient legacy. He'd never heard of tribal queens or princesses, but anything was possible. Even if she turned out to be the hostile leader's mistress, it would still be vital leverage.

Aguirre made his move, advancing on her blind side as the woman moved away from him. He would approach her from behind and wait until he had her covered before speaking, maybe club her down without a verbal warning. Anything to give him the advantage.

He would never know what tipped the woman to his presence, but she turned when he was still some thirty feet behind her, stealthily advancing. First she blinked at him, then clearly recognized him as a stranger, leveling her M-16. Aguirre raised his own and called for her surrender in his native Spanish.

When she shot him, it was a complete surprise. He saw the muzzle-flash and felt the bullets rip into his abdomen. He was lying on his back before he had a chance to fire in return. Another moment, and the woman loomed above him, peering at Aguirre's face.

It was peculiar, but he could have sworn she was surprised, as well. She blinked at him, holding her weapon pointed at his face, but even through his bleary eyes Aguirre saw her finger wasn't resting on the trigger.

Strange, he thought. There ought to be more pain.

And thinking it, the treasure hunter died.

26

Night's cloak covered Site X as Bolan bounded down the mossy stairs. A young guerrilla stepped out of the shadows at their bottom, angling his piece toward Bolan, but a short burst from the Steyr put him on his back. The Executioner leaped over him, kept going, looking for the hot eye of the storm.

The GPLF men were everywhere, ducking and running, firing into doorways, strafing shadows. Bolan heard another loud crack from the Springfield, toward the site's southern perimeter, and wondered whether any of his other short-term friends were still alive.

They hadn't come prepared for this, although it might've been anticipated once their adversaries were identified. He reckoned some of them would die, perhaps the lot, and wondered if the folks they left behind would think the sacrifice worthwhile.

He cleared the structure where he'd made his roost before the battle started, moving toward the city's central pyramid. Gunfire echoed on every side, but much of it seemed to be aimless fire triggered by frightened youths who lacked a solid target. Bolan thought he might as well add more confusion to the mix.

He paused in shadow, ready for his last spring over weed-choked ground to reach the pyramid. He took the detonator from his pocket. Bolan still had seven fist-sized C-4 charges planted at strategic points throughout the ancient city. None of them had been adjacent to the hiding places of his comrades when the shooting started, and he'd shown the others where they were, in case the natives had to move as he had done. They should be safe—assuming they were still alive— but Bolan couldn't track them down and check.

Choosing the packet farthest from him, on the north rim of the site, he sent a signal beaming through the night and watched it blow. An orange blossom of flame unfurled its petals, searing anyone within a radius of twenty feet and spraying stony shrapnel.

Bolan didn't know if anyone had been within the C-4's killing range, and he had no time to investigate the blast site. He was busy lighting up the town.

His second charge was closer, more to the northwest. Again he thumbed the radio-remote control. Again a shock wave shuddered through the Mayan settlement. This time, the cries of wounded men were audible behind it, telling Bolan that the blast had not been wasted energy.

Instead of following the counterclockwise chain around Site X, he switched to blow the next charge on his southern flank. It was the closest yet, no more than thirty yards away, but screened from Bolan by the stout bulk of the pyramid. His only glimpse of the explosion was a glimmer of reflected firelight, there and gone, but he could hear it well enough.

More screams.

Four charges left to go.

A dazed guerrilla almost stumbled into Bolan, reeling toward him from the darkness, clutching at his bloody abdomen with one hand while his rifle dangled from the other. On his heels, one of the villagers on Bolan's team sprang forward, brandishing a razor-edged machete. The guerrilla spun to face his enemy, raising his M-16, and Bolan put a single 5.56 mm mangler through his skull. The Indian saluted Bolan with his knife, let out a yelp of thanks, and doubled back in the direction he had come from, seeking other prey.

The battle couldn't last much longer, Bolan knew, if it was

hand-to-hand already. Then again, perhaps the Indian with the machete had been one of those who had no gun to start with. Bolan couldn't tell from one glimpse in the night, and he had other pressing matters on his mind.

Four charges remained, and thirty-odd guerrillas left to kill, at least.

He keyed a C-4 charge due east of where he sheltered in the shadows, saw and felt its blast rip through the jungle night. For a split second the illumination showed him bodies airborne, tumbling like crash-test dummies, then the light winked out again, leaving its afterimage on his retinas.

More hostiles down. Three charges left.

He broke from cover, jogging toward the pyramid, and simultaneously triggered two more blasts to cover his advance. A swirl of dust and smoke enveloped Bolan, wafting through the camp, smelling of death and cordite. Men were shouting, cursing, screaming all around him.

Bolan understood none of it but the screams.

It seemed that he had heard them all his life.

PACO ALVAREZ DREW his hand back from his face and scowled at the blood on his palm. More dribbled down his jaw and soaked into the collar of his worn fatigue shirt, but he didn't think the wound was critical.

An arrow, for the love of God!

It had come hurtling from the darkness, nothing but a blur sucking the whisper-stream along behind it. Then the impact rocked him like a hard punch to the face, while blazing agony enveloped his cheek and jaw. He'd known that it was not a bullet, even as he reached up blindly, gripped the feathered shaft and tore it from his cheek, clenching his teeth around the scream.

A goddamned arrow in his face!

He gave the archer credit, then decided that the shot was probably a lucky accident. Still reeling from the blow, Alvarez found that he could barely see through his right eye, although the orb itself had not been injured. Pain beyond description flooded it with tears, and when he wiped it with his free hand he made matters worse, smearing the lids with blood.

Two inches up and over, and he would've lost the eye. Three inches, and he would've been a dead man lying on the ancient pavement with an arrow through his skull, ants scuttling in his blood.

It was too close for comfort, but he wasn't finished yet. The scar might even help him with the ladies—those who liked their lovers rough and rugged—but before he got around to romance Alvarez still had a job to do.

Three jobs, in fact.

Killing his enemies, looting the treasure site, and burying the slaves he had dragooned to help him with the second part.

He yearned to kill the archer who had wounded him but couldn't trace the arrow if his life depended on it. All was chaos in the Mayan city, with his soldiers running every which way, firing aimlessly, their enemies concealed in darkness while the place reverberated with explosions here, there, everywhere.

It all reminded Alvarez of Hell, part of the afterlife which he had disavowed in college, when he still knew everything about the universe and all its mysteries. He knew a great deal less today and wasn't truly sure of anything except the cause he served with every fiber of his being.

And in truth, he had begun to question even that.

Reeling with pain, leaving a trail of blood with every step, he broke from cover, took another route around the crumbling structure that had sheltered him, in case the archer wasn't merely lucky but was waiting for him to appear once more. The bastard wouldn't get a second chance if Alvarez had anything to say about it.

His simple plan of sweeping through the city, driving all his enemies before him, had disintegrated when explosions started ripping through the ranks and scattering his men in panic. Alvarez had no plan now, except to stay alive, rally whichever men he could, and kill their enemies wherever he could find them in the ruins.

Simple.

Except that he was wounded, his men were running wild without a trace of discipline, and Alvarez had no clue where to find their adversaries in the dark.

He drifted through the ruins, praying that a target would present itself before blood loss and pain rendered him helpless. Once, he thought he'd found one, but he held his fire another second to be sure and realized that he had nearly killed one of his own.

Chaos.

They'd never drilled for anything resembling the present situation, focusing instead on ambushes and booby traps, patrols and individual assassinations. Alvarez had never contemplated anything like this, but he would not forget it if he ever had the opportunity to train another team.

The second time he spied a target, Alvarez suppressed the rush of excitement. It was likely one of his again, disoriented in the darkness and—

Even with one bad eye and only moonlight to illuminate the scene, he realized that he was looking at a *woman* with a rifle in her hands. And if that was not surprise enough, Alvarez recognized her face.

It was the bitch who had escaped from him the night before last, with her native guide! The archaeologist, or so she'd claimed. Her weapon did not strike him as a scientific instrument, but Alvarez cared nothing for the many lies that she had told him.

All he wanted was revenge.

It would've been an easy shot, even one-eyed, but Alvarez decided that mere death delivered from a distance was too quick and merciful. His bad luck had begun the day he'd met this woman in the forest, and he meant to make her pay for each misfortune that he'd suffered since that time.

Smiling with half his blood-smeared visage, Alvarez fell into step behind her, hastening to close the gap.

CARRIE TRAVIS HAD no idea of how to navigate a modern battlefield. If the events had taken place five hundred or a thousand years ago, she would've known precisely what to do—marking the field, scanning for artifacts, cautiously excavating anything she found—but it was altogether different with the combatants still alive and fighting.

Altogether deadly.

When she stopped to think about it, only for a fraction of a second at a time, Travis was startled that she didn't feel remorse for having killed a man she'd never met before. It was survival of the fittest, kill or be killed, and she'd done what was required to stay alive.

Guilt might come later, when she had time to reflect, but at the moment she was still primarily concerned with living. And with finding Matt Cooper.

Where was he? Was he even still alive?

She couldn't picture Cooper dead—he seemed too strong and competent for that—but strong, competent men died every day. That thought drove needles of despair into her heart, because she sensed that her survival depended on the stranger who had saved her once and might do so again, if he was able.

And if not, at least she had her rifle.

Travis had examined it briefly after the first shooting, and she'd discovered how to drop an empty magazine. Since then, she had collected several spares from bodies found along her way, stuffing her pockets until she felt dressed to kill.

Within the past few minutes there'd been two occasions when she could've killed again, but Travis had abstained. She understood that they were enemies, trying to kill her friends, but something stopped her when she raised the rifle to her shoulder, sighting down its barrel at a stranger's back. If either target had been facing her, firing at her, then Travis knew she would've fired, but as it was…

I've let them down, she thought. Maybe I've killed them.

What if one of the guerrillas she had spared went on to kill Luis Candera or Matt Cooper? What if they wiped out her tiny group of native allies? How could she live with that?

I couldn't, she decided.

And it wouldn't matter, since she'd doubtless die soon afterward, eliminated with the rest.

Travis had reached the junction of two ancient streets, weeds sprouting through and all around the massive, crumbling stones. Three rebels hammered past her, running all-out for who knew where, as if their lives depended on it. Watching them from hiding, Travis realized that she had no idea where she was going or what she would do in the event that she found Cooper still alive.

He plainly didn't want her with him while the battle was in progress. That was clear enough when he told her to run away, stressing that he could spare no time to babysit a helpless woman while their enemies were breathing down his neck. Cooper had granted her an escort, dead now, and insisted in effect that she should stay out of his way.

What am I doing here? she thought.

The answer to that question took more thought than she could spare. Confused and angry, Travis changed her mind about locating Cooper and decided she would give him what he wanted. She would get out of his life once and for all.

But which way should she go?

The epicenter of the fighting lay before her, eddies of it swirling brutally to left and right. Her nearest access to the jungle lay behind her. Once she reached the trees and darkness, she could find a place to hide and wait to see who won the contest—or she could strike off alone, while her opponents were distracted by Cooper and the rest.

Do it! she told herself. You may not get another chance!

Turning, she found a rifle pointed at her face from barely three feet distant. Blood masked half the shooter's face, but when he spoke she recognized the voice.

"Put down the gun," Paco Alvarez said.

27

The two guerrillas spotted Bolan just as he saw them. They knew him for an enemy at once, and they were bent on killing him.

They might've done it, too, if not for just a heartbeat's hesitation.

Bolan did not hesitate. He hit them with a figure-eight burst from the hip, stitching the gunman on his left first, then the carbon-copy target on his right. They each got off a few stray rounds as they were toppling over backward, but the slugs came nowhere close to Bolan.

He was moving by the time they hit the ground, scanning the battlefield for enemies and friends alike.

The layout was unique in Bolan's long experience. He'd fought in tropic jungles and in urban ones, but never had the two combined like this, with looming structures overgrown by vegetation, offering a kind of twilight zone between two worlds.

Still it was fitting, he decided, since the Mayans had been avid fans of human sacrifice. If any of their ghosts were watching, they'd be overjoyed by all the bloodletting.

A hunting party emerged from the shadows, five guerrillas moving furtively despite their numbers, trying hard to watch all directions at once while they moved through the hellgrounds. Bolan crouched against the north wall of a building he could not identify and checked the Steyr's clear plastic magazine. He still had twenty-three of his first forty-two rounds remaining and judged that it should be enough.

Setting the piece for 3-round bursts, he found a target, framed it in his sights and stroked the rifle's trigger. He had picked the hunting party's rear guard for a reason, closing the back door behind them with his first rounds, urging them to move in his direction when the last man in their ragged line went down.

And so it played.

His bullets dropped the human target in a twisted sprawl of arms and legs. The two guerrillas nearest to the dear departed started hammering full-auto fire in opposite directions, clueless as to where the lethal rounds had come from. Bolan took them with a one-two punch that put them down and kept them there.

And that left two.

One of the hunters had glimpsed Bolan's muzzle-flash. He came on strong, showing more guts than brains with his impulsive rush. Bolan drilled both—the guts and the brains with rising bursts that stitched his adversary from his groin to his forehead. Concussive impact punched the shooter back onto his rump, leaving him stretched out in the weeds.

And that left one.

The hunting party's sole survivor turned and ran. It would've been an easy thing to let him slide, but Bolan couldn't read the shooter's mind to know if he would run all night or stop within a hundred yards and double back to fight again. Bolan took the shot, three 5.56 mm shockers shattering the rebel's spine and dumping him facedown outside the entrance to a looted tomb.

Rising, Bolan was switching off his nearly empty magazine for a replacement when he heard a woman's voice raised in protest, a sound that came and went on crackling waves of gunfire, almost an illusion.

Was he hearing things?

He took a chance and moved in the direction of the sound, hoping that it might be repeated, holding to his course when it was not. Avoiding contact with his GPLF adversaries for the moment, Bolan stalked the memory of words he hadn't understood, homing on the approximate location where he thought they had originated.

He arrived in time to catch a glimpse of Carrie Travis in the clutches of a gunman masked with blood, the right side of his face a crimson ruin. The guerrilla grasped the archaeologist's right arm with his left hand, holding his rifle in the right as he propelled her toward the shadows of a nearby building draped with vines and creepers.

Bolan followed, double-timing over ancient grass and ancient stones turned murky crimson by the blood from scattered corpses. None of those he passed were members of his tiny squad, as far as he could tell. Travis and her unwelcome escort disappeared around a corner, but he reached it swiftly, hesitated long enough to listen for the panting sounds of struggle, then stepped out to join them.

Paco Alvarez, half-drenched in blood from what appeared to be a ragged face wound, had apparently knocked Travis to the ground, leaving her stunned. He was engaged in tearing at her clothes when Bolan spoke his name from ten feet back. The sound arrested any further moves toward Travis, quelled whatever mixture of desire and rage had motivated Alvarez to snatch her in the first place, focusing his full attention on the Executioner.

Bolan allowed his enemy to rise, lifting his M-16 with an uncomfortable grip around its plastic stock. There'd be a heartbeat's fumbling hesitation if he tried to clutch the pistol grip, and Bolan had him covered as it was.

"How do you know me?" Alvarez inquired. "I don't know you."

"You're famous, Paco," Bolan told him. "Though I have to say, your photographs don't do you justice. Love the makeover."

Alvarez flashed a twisted smile.

"It was an arrow. You believe that, gringo?"

"Never mind. I'll fix it for you," Bolan said.

"You came to get the treasure, eh?"

"Just keeping it from you," Bolan replied.

"With this one, sure." Alvarez kept his eyes on Bolan as he tipped a nod toward Travis. "All you Yankees stick together."

"This is getting old," Bolan said. "Shall we do this thing, or what?"

"You're right." The rebel forced another ghastly smile. "I do you first, then her."

His awkward grip prevented Alvarez from having much chance with the M-16. He was still fumbling with it when a 3-round burst from Bolan's rifle ripped through his chest and tipped him over in a lifeless sprawl.

Travis lunged forward, grabbing the dead man's rifle. Bolan saw the extra magazines protruding from her pockets as she spoke.

"All right," she said. "I'm ready."

Bolan shook his head, then told her, "All right, then. Come on."

THE GUNFIRE from the ancient city's ruins had begun to falter, slowing, becoming more sporadic. After twenty minutes of frenetic action, it appeared to Alejandro Cruz that it would soon be over.

What he couldn't tell, as yet, was which side would emerge victorious.

Cruz knew that many of his men were dead. There had been gunfire from at least two unfamiliar weapons, plus the series of explosions he could not explain. None of his troops carried grenades, much less charges of high explosives. Someone else had mined the city, and his men had rushed into the trap.

On my orders, he thought, a sickly feeling creeping over him.

Cruz glanced back at the sullen villagers, all thirty-five of them still under guard by half a dozen of his troops whom he'd withheld from combat in the ruins. Would those six have made the difference? Or did the others even need them?

Cruz imagined losing everything—not just the Mayan treasure, but the hard core of his private army and his reputation, possibly his life. It seemed impossible that everything he'd worked and fought for through the years could all come crashing down around him in a single night, but that was how things happened in a war. Napoleon took a wrong turn at Waterloo. Hitler ignored the calendar and blundered into Russia with cruel winter coming on. The Yankees slept on Sunday morning, at Pearl Harbor.

If he lost everything, Crūz knew that it would be his fault. He could blame others, but he would be lying to himself. Since rising to command the movement he had held the reins in strong, unyielding hands. Each major decision was his, including that which sucked them into dealing with Aguirre and relying on the ancient gold he'd offered like resplendent bait for an insidious and deadly trap.

It was too late to rewrite history or moan about his choices. Cruz had to play the cards that he'd been dealt—those he had dealt himself—stay to watch the final moments of the game.

Whether he won or lost, Cruz wouldn't have it said that he had run away.

There was a restless shifting in the ranks of his unsettled hostages, a murmuring among them that Cruz didn't like. "Silence!" he raged at them, clutching his M-16 against his chest.

A rock sailed through the night and made him duck, a near-miss that would probably have stunned him if it had connected. Instantly, a couple of his men began clubbing the nearest hostages with their gun butts, while others kept their distance, covering the crowd.

It happened swiftly, startling Cruz with yet another lesson in how quickly things could fall apart. One of the peasants lunged and grabbed the barrel of the nearest sentry's rifle, yanking on it, pulling Cruz's man off balance. Even as the soldier fired into his chest, dropping the reckless villager, three others rushed and bore him to the ground beneath their writhing, thrashing weight.

And instantly, the crowd of hostages became a seething mob. They overran his soldiers, deaf to gunfire, heedless of the bullets ripping into some of them. There were enough to drag all six of Cruz's shooters down and smother them in flesh, while angry fingers gouged their eyes and clamped around their throats.

Cruz fired into the surging mass of bodies, caring not at all if he shot man, woman or child. When three or four had fallen, half the mob abruptly turned and rushed him, howling at him with a single outraged voice.

Cruz turned and ran.

His only avenue of exit was the ruined city, where his soldiers still fought for their lives. At least he had friends there, and they had weapons. Some of them would see him and defend him from the lynch-mad peasants on his heels.

"Help me!" Cruz shouted as he fled into the ruins. "Someone help me, please!"

"WHAT'S THAT?" Travis asked.

Bolan paused to listen. While shots still echoed through the Mayan city, there was something else. At first, it sounded like the rush of floodwaters over a rocky bed of stones, but then he recognized it was the melded voice of fury from a mob.

"Somebody's coming," he replied, and nodded toward the broad steps of the city's central pyramid, immediately to their left. "Let's take the high ground."

"Right."

Travis kept pace with him, knees pumping as she climbed. Bolan was only two long strides ahead of her when he crested the summit, moving toward the south face of the pyramid and staring out across the ruined city.

There, some forty yards away and sixty feet below him,

Bolan saw a lone man running from pursuers. He counted some two dozen of them, recognizing several in the front ranks from Candera's village. What had brought them to the city Bolan couldn't say, but from their violent fury toward the GPLF's leader he could guess.

"Who's that?" Travis asked, standing at his elbow.

"The guy in front is Alejandro Cruz, head of the Guatemalan People's Liberation Front. You met the others yesterday."

"Luis's people? But—"

Before she had the chance to ask another question, Cruz spun to confront the mob, firing a burst that raked its foremost rank and dropped four of the villagers before his magazine ran dry. The others hit Cruz like a cresting wave and drove him back against the stone steps of the pyramid, flailing at him with their fists, feet and whatever foreign objects they'd picked up along the way.

"They'll kill him," Travis said.

"I wouldn't be surprised."

"Oh, well."

She met his gaze for just a moment, as she turned away, then moved back toward the center of the pyramid's flat roof, where she would not be forced to watch.

Bolan stayed where he was and saw it through.

Midway through the dismantling of Alejandro Cruz, he heard the helicopters coming. Faint at first, then growing louder as they closed from the southwest. Closing his eyes, Bolan guessed two, perhaps three military choppers, likely U.S. Army-surplus Hueys large enough to carry ten or fifteen soldiers each.

"I hear something," Travis said, coming back to join him.

"That would be the cavalry," Bolan said.

"So, your call worked after all."

"Something got through," he stated.

"Hey, that's good." She searched his face, then added, "Right?"

"It's good for you," he answered. "My advice would be to ditch the rifle and the magazines. Just pitch them down the steps and wait right here. The choppers will have spotlights. You don't want the gunners to mistake you for a rebel."

"Right," she said, sounding confused. "Okay. What about you?"

"I won't be here," he told her.

"But—"

"I had a job to do," Bolan said, "and it's done. Don't make more of it than it is."

"I wouldn't dream of it," she answered. Spinning suddenly, like an Olympic discus thrower, Travis pitched her M-16 into the night. The spare clips followed, clattering as they bounced on the steps below.

"There," she said. "Satisfied?"

"You should be fine," he said, turning away from her.

"What should I tell them?" Travis asked his back.

"Whatever you like," Bolan said, on the move. "They'll make up something, anyway."

He reached the stairs and started down. Travis ran to stand above him, at the edge, and called down after him, "Will I see you again?"

"Don't count on it," the Executioner replied, already halfway down the steps.

"All right," he heard her say before the night enfolded him. "I won't."

He was a quarter mile into the jungle, moving through the night like any other predator, before the helicopters thundered overhead and kept on going, leaving him behind as they sped toward the killing ground.

Epilogue

Guatemala City

Hal Brognola answered on the first ring, as if he'd been sitting by the telephone. But then, considering the time in Washington, he probably had been.

"When are you coming back?" he asked, when they'd engaged their scramblers and disposed of the amenities.

"Another couple days," Bolan replied. "I want to keep an eye on things down here. Make sure they don't go wrong."

"She's fine," Brognola said, cutting directly to the chase as usual.

"You checked?" Bolan asked.

"And I'm not the only one. Seems Stanford University's been burning up the phone lines, getting California's senators and congress people up in arms."

"I thought she was from Princeton," Bolan said.

"The father was. They went bicoastal. Anyway, I put my two cents in for Justice, and from what I understand somebody at the White House made a call. She has a couple of Marines for babysitters, and the embassy is jumping through all kinds of hoops."

"No charges, then?" Bolan asked.

"Charges? Hell, I wouldn't be surprised if she came out of it with medals. Maybe honorary citizenship. The government's so happy to have Cruz and Alvarez in body bags, they can't decide whether to call a holiday or finish mopping up the People's Liberation Front. My guess would be they mop up first, then celebrate."

"Sounds wise to me," Bolan observed.

"And then you've got Site X," Brognola said, "which they're calling the find of the century. Archaeologists will by picking over it for years, maybe decades. What I hear, the Travis woman's got a bid in to participate and maybe lead the dig. There's fifty or a hundred miles of red tape that she'll have to wade through first, but after all the coverage I can't see how they'd keep her off the team."

"That's good," Bolan said. "It was all she wanted, really."

"So, now that you're finished down there," Brognola said.

The Executioner waited to hear where the next battle in his War Everlasting would take him.

RED FROST

Stony Man prepares for the worst when a Russian
nuclear submarine inexplicably runs aground near
Seattle. But the worst becomes unthinkable when an
army of ex–Spetsnaz troops seeks revenge for the
lost honor of the once-mighty Soviet war machine.

STONY® MAN

*Available August
wherever
you buy books.*

Or order your copy now by sending your name, address, zip or postal code, along with a check or
money order (please do not send cash) for $6.50 for each book ordered ($7.99 in Canada), plus
75¢ postage and handling ($1.00 in Canada), payable to Gold Eagle Books, to:

In the U.S.	In Canada
Gold Eagle Books	Gold Eagle Books
3010 Walden Avenue	P.O. Box 636
P.O. Box 9077	Fort Erie, Ontario
Buffalo, NY 14269-9077	L2A 5X3

Please specify book title with your order.
Canadian residents add applicable federal and provincial taxes.

**GOLD
EAGLE** ®

GSM90

JAMES AXLER

DEATH LANDS®

Remember
Tomorrow

An earthquake in the Arkansas dust bowls shakes up the warriors, leaving an amnesic J. B. Dix in the employ of the iron-fisted ruler of Duma. Can Ryan and the others save their friend from the most dangerous ville in all the Deathlands?

Available September wherever you buy books.

JAKE STRAIT

TWIST OF CAIN

BY FRANK RICH

Jake Strait has been hired by one of the rich and powerful to find an elusive serial killer, who is handy with a nail gun and is a collector of body parts. Except Jake Strait has been set up from the start.

Available in October wherever books are sold.